TONYA KAPPES

A
Charming
Hex

Magical Cures Mystery Series
Book nine

Acknowledgements

To my Krew members. Gosh. We've come a long day from June burning her shed in her back yard in Locust Grove. I couldn't write June without y'all in my head and encouraging me through emails and social media. I truly love you all. Thank you from the bottom of my heart.

Sam McCarthy is a rock star! I asked my readers to help me name a what-knot shop and Sam came up with Hidden Treasures. It's perfect for Whispering Falls! You will get a little introduction to Hidden Treasures in A Charming Hex. I just love it.

Thank you to Cyndy Ranzau. You are the best editor anyone could ask for. You go above and beyond for not only me, but June Heal and bringing her adventures to the page! This has been a fun journey, girl!

Of course I have to give a shout out to my family of now men. When I started writing June, my boys were in elementary, middle, and high school. Now three are in college while the last one is a senior in high school. They have grown up with June and sees her as just another member of the family. I love you guys! And Eddy…who doesn't love him? He's so patient and kind as I spend many night, days, and weekends pouring June's life story out on the computer. He says he loves seeing me smile as I type. He is the love of my life.

Welcome back Whispering Falls.

Xo

Tonya

Chapter One

Ahh, the long and much needed sigh passed my lips. I lifted my chin up to the warm tropical sun and dug my toes in the hot, grainy sand. I'd never been to the beach. Darla never took me on a summer vacation. She said that the tourists ruined the natural habitats and she didn't want my images of Earth's natural beauty to be tainted at an early age, and that I had all my life to be influenced by outside forces she couldn't control when I became of age.

But I couldn't help but think that she'd love being here with me right now.

The crystal blue and almost white water was very calm. The small waves curled slightly over the sand, creeping up and hitting the tiptop of my toes. I smiled and glanced down the beach in both directions. No one was there. Just me and the white sand surrounding me as far as the eye could see.

"Oscar?" The flailing arms in the ocean caught my attention. Where was Oscar? "Oscar?" I pushed myself up to stand, not even worried about the hot sand that felt like a bed of hot rocks on the soles of my feet.

The arms went under and my instincts kicked in.

I dove into the vast ocean, surprised it was so deep as soon as I took my first step. Deeper and deeper I pushed myself, from the crystal blue into the suddenly-turning black, dark depths of the ocean with the arms of the man in sight.

A bright orange light pierced the darkness and dove in a spiral around the man. The man's body stiffened, his arms out to the side, his head thrown back, and his eyes looking over at me.

The water felt as if it turned to ice, my body was still warm, but the man's glare chilled the space between us. His eyes were diamonds. I watched as the spiral closed—he was gone. The spiral was gone. I pushed myself up toward the surface. The ice surrounded me. It sucked the air out of my lungs. I pushed harder, fighting the heaviness in my chest.

The light. The light of the bright sun pierced the surface of the water.

Just a little more. Push to the top. My mind told my body, but my arms were stuck to my sides as if there were concrete blocks tied to each finger. My shoulders moved rapidly back and forth. I kicked my legs. The light wasn't far, but the blackness engulfed me.

"Ahhh!" The animalistic sound escaped me from deep inside as I gasped for air.

"June." I heard the familiar voice and felt the strong hand stroke my back. "It's just a dream. Just a dream. Open your eyes. Please open your eyes."

When I tried to open my eyes, my inhale skipped down my nose and filled my lungs. The darkness filled with light as my body willed my eyes open.

"Oh, baby." Oscar pulled me into his safe and warm arms after my eyes found his face. His crystal blue eyes held concern. "It's okay," he assured me. He rubbed his strong hand down the back of my head as it rested against his chest.

"The beach." The words came out in a raspy voice as though my mouth was filled with the sand that I had just dreamed my toes were in. "There was a man drowning."

That was all I could remember. My nightmares were so intense, I swear my body and mind blocked the memories.

One problem, I knew over the course of a few days, the memories would trickle back into my head and leave me with the memory of the full dream. And sometimes it was too late. I'd never had a nightmare where some part of it hadn't come true.

"You are just stressed," he assured me. "You've never been to the beach and you're not sure what to expect, but I promise," his heartbeat thundered in his chest; I pressed my ear closer to him, "I promise, we are going to have a wonderful time."

"I really think I need to take Mr. Prince Charming," I whispered and pulled away. I glanced around the room looking for my fairy-god cat.

"June," Oscar's head tilted. His hair was stuck up in different directions all over his head and as black as a raven's wing. "It's our honeymoon. Nothing is going to happen to us. I am a cop. I can protect us."

"But. . ." I gulped knowing that whenever I had a nightmare like the one I had just had, something evil was lurking.

"But nothing." He pulled the covers back and pushed himself up with his muscular arms and got out of bed. "I'm going to get in the shower. Don't be late for the council meeting."

I watched him disappear out the bedroom door. I waited until I heard the water turn on and the shower curtain pulled close before I reached over and rubbed the palm of my hand over the glass crystal ball of my other familiar, Madame Torres.

"Who is it that you seek? Or shall I say who seeks you?" The voice dripped out of the confines of the ball.

"I am open to who seeks me or the dangers surrounding my dreams." I could feel the fear in my voice as it trickled through my vocal cords.

I closed my eyes and let all the sounds and the feelings of the dream drift away from my soul. When I opened my eyes, Madame Torres had turned her ball into a clear calcite crystal. The small bubbles floated deep within her. My eyes focused on the center of her. The answer within the depth of Madame Torres told me everything I needed to know.

"Mr. Prince Charming," her voice was resigned.

Meow, meow. Mr. Prince Charming yawned. He was curled up in a tight ball at the foot of the bed.

My white, ornery fairy-god cat reached his front legs out in front of him, elongating his arms and spread his claws apart before his entire body waved in full stretch.

I tried to swallow the lump that had formed in my throat.

The clear calcite turned lavender and Madame Torres's face appeared, taking up most of the space within her ball. The orange turban perched on her head had a large diamond in the front where the material was gathered, bringing the memory of the man's eyes from my nightmare back into my head.

The waves deep in the ball moved like those of the ocean. Her eyes magnified, the bright yellow eye shadow covered her lids, bright red rogue was rubbed along her cheekbones, her lips stained ruby red.

"Mr. Prince Charming must accompany you and Oscar on your honeymoon." Madame Torres was well aware that Mr. Prince Charming was the last familiar Oscar wanted me to bring. Plus it wasn't easy trying to get a cat on a plane or to a tropical island. "Or you shall not go."

"So you do see some sort of danger?" I had to clarify. "We shouldn't go on the honeymoon?"

"What?" Oscar walked into the bedroom with a towel around his waist and another one in his hand dragging it through his wet hair. "We are going on a honeymoon. I'm taking you to the beach and we are going to be secluded. No one around but us. And no magic."

"Madame Torres said that. . ." I pointed to her but kept my eyes on his handsome physique.

"Madame Torres hasn't been outside of Whispering Falls and wants to go." Oscar sat on the bed and leaned toward my familiar.

The only thing he could see was her lavender liquid insides rolling around. He didn't have the gift of reading crystal balls. Oscar was a wizard and he only knew how to use his wand. But I could see the look on Madame Torres's face as she glared and then rolled her eyes in his direction. I smiled. Neither of my familiars got along well with my husband. I felt like I was constantly brokering peace between them.

"I'm going to head to Locust Grove and finish up my paperwork so we can be on the plane in the morning," he said in a stern voice. "Don't you think I'm a nervous wreck about flying? I've been to the beach a bunch but we always drove." He sat down on the edge of the bed next to me. "You are nervous about flying in a plane." He kissed my forehead. "It's really fun. I've flown several times and you are going to love it. Promise." He criss-crossed his heart with his finger.

Rowl. Mr. Prince Charming wasn't happy with Oscar's observation. He batted at us and darted off the bed.

I patted Madame Torres on the top of her ball when Oscar left the bedroom. I peeled the covers off me and got out of bed. There was so much to do before Oscar and I left and staying in bed worried about a nightmare that may or may not come true wasn't going to check the to-do items off my list.

I tooled around my cottage and got ready for the day while I waited for my coffee to brew. I loved where I lived.

It was small and cozy. It had only one bedroom and bath along with the family room and a kitchen. But the view was undeniably the best feature. I leaned over the kitchen sink and stared out the window, overlooking the magical town I called home. Whispering Falls, Kentucky.

The morning sun was dripping over the mountains and spotlighting all the cozy shops that held secrets only the members of the village understood. Like Oscar, everyone who lived in Whispering Falls had a magical power. In mortal words we'd be called witches. In our world we considered ourselves Spiritualists.

My homeopathic cure shop, A Charming Cure, was my cover for my spiritual gift of potion making. It was a gift I had gotten from my spiritual side of the family—my father's side. I grew up in Locust Grove, a neighboring town about twenty minutes away, with non-spiritualist Darla, my mother who didn't like to be referred to as Ms. Heal, Miss Heal, Mrs. Heal, or Mom. So I called her Darla. She was a mortal and tried to use my father's family journal to create homeopathic cures, but it wasn't until she died and I got my hands on the journal did the recipes come to life.

Growing up, Oscar and I lived next door to each other in Locust Grove and it wasn't until we were in our mid-twenties that Isadora Solstice came to Locust Grove and told us of our real heritage, along with introducing us to the magical village of Whispering Falls. It was here that we embraced our gifts and made it our home. Oscar was a police officer in both Locust Grove and Whispering Falls. It wasn't until a few months ago that we finally got married, but had yet to take a honeymoon.

It was easy for mortals to drop everything and go on a honeymoon, but it was different for us. Well. . .for me. My two familiars kept me safe from the outside forces and knew things before they happened. The nightmare for instance. I didn't have them a lot, but when I did, I had to be on high alert. I couldn't help but think I was having one because I was leaving the comforts of our small town like Oscar had said.

"I can't worry about the what if's," I said and poured myself a hot cup of coffee to go and made a mental note to grab some Mr. Sandman Sprinkles from my shop. Mr. Sandman was the best potion I had created to help me sleep. Though. . .I'd promised Oscar "no magic" on the honeymoon, but I was sure sanity trumped it.

Mewl, Mr. Prince Charming was perched on the back of the couch. He walked it like a tightrope and jumped off at the end. He stood at the front door. When I opened it, he darted out and down the hill toward Whispering Falls. His tail swayed back and forth. He was on a mission. I shook my head and locked the door behind me. He was like an old man in the village. Every morning he made his rounds to all the shops and greeted them.

Mr. Prince Charming had shown up on my porch in Locust Grove on my tenth birthday. I knew he wasn't a present from Darla. We didn't do birthday presents. We barely did cake. It was the only time Darla would let me eat sweets.

That particular year, the cake Darla had gotten me had *Happy Retirement Stu* written on it along with the manager's special sticker on it. Darla hadn't even bothered scrapping off Stu's name.

Mr. Prince Charming showed up with a dingy collar and a turtle charm that was missing an eye. Oscar gave me his mom's old bracelet for the charm. It was the best birthday I'd ever had.

I ran my hand over my wrist and felt my charm bracelet, bringing me out of my thoughts.

"See," I said out loud. "If I really were in danger, Mr. Prince Charming would've given me another charm."

I took a close look at all the charms he'd given me for protection. I was fine. I was safe. But I was still stressed and needed a June's Gem.

Just thinking about the chocolaty treat made my mouth water and I knew I had to make a pit stop at Wicked Good Bakery before I went to my shop. Without much more thought, I let my stomach and stress guide me and before I knew it, I was standing on the sidewalk right in front of Wicked Good Bakery.

Raven Mortimer was inside her bakery working away behind the counter and getting ready for the morning rush when Wicked Good opened. The green and pink awning above the shop windows flapped in the morning breeze.

Lightly I tapped on the door and got her attention. Raven's long black hair was pulled up in a ponytail; the Wicked Good apron was almost white from all the flour doused on it. She was rolling out dough, kneading it and shaping it when she looked up. A big grin scrolled up to her eyes. She rubbed her hands across the front of the apron before she walked over and unlocked the door.

"Get in here." She pushed the door open and hurried back behind the counter. "If I don't get these in the oven, I won't have a dang thing for my customers to purchase."

"Thank you for letting me borrow Faith. I know she does all your deliveries and works around here." Faith Mortimer was Raven's sister. She worked for Raven part-time at the bakery, full-time as the editor-in-chief of the *Whispering Falls Gazette*, and part-time for me at A Charming Cure. Faith was going to work at the shop the entire time I was gone. "I'm so glad I don't have to close the shop for the honeymoon."

I gestured to one of the June's Gems she took out of the oven. It was her take on the Ding Dong and was named after me. She nodded.

"Are you getting excited?" she asked just as I took a bite of the savory cake.

"Mmm." I tilted my head side-to-side, my ears to my shoulders in a "meh" kind of way. After I swallowed, I said, "I had one of my nightmares last night."

"Really?" she asked and then scanned her eyes down her pastry counter. "I don't see anything here." She referred to her spiritual gift of Aleuromancy. She was able to see signs in her work, the dough. She made the most wonderful fortune cookies. She had a gift of putting in just the exact right fortune the customer needed.

"Good." I wiped across my mouth with the back of my hand. "That's a good thing."

"It sure is." Raven smiled and went back to kneading the ball of dough in front of her. "Faith is so excited to be in charge of the shop. She said she's going to redo the display window with a fun summer theme."

"That's what I love about her. She does whatever she wants." I pointed to another June's Gem. She nodded again.

"It's not like you to eat two, you must be stressed," she noted. "If I see anything before you leave, I'll be sure to let you know."

"Great." I grabbed one of the Wicked Good to-go bags and put the June's Gem in it. "This will make a great snack for before the meeting."

It was true. Ding Dongs were and are my stress-relieving treat. Raven invented the June's Gems and right now I was stressed out to the max.

"That's right!" She smacked the dough down on to the counter, flatting it out before she took the rolling pin doused in flour and flatted the dough more. "You find out from the village council where you get to go on your honeymoon."

"You know." I wagged my finger in the air and walked backward to the door. "Growing up as a mortal I had always envisioned my wedding. It was nothing like I had planned. Then I also had this idea in my head about my honeymoon." I shook my head. "I never imagined I'd be letting a group full of witches figure out where I was going to go." I referred to the council meeting today.

The village council had called a special meeting to decide where Oscar and I could go on our honeymoon. We were able to send in a list of destinations. Of course I wrote down Hawaii and Oscar wrote down Jamaica. Both of us wanted to go to a beach, that was for sure.

We were excited to find out which one they picked. Really either was good with me. Toes in the sand and a drink in my hand was how I was going to spend my much-needed week-long vacation.

"You're lucky." She wagged her brows up and down. She and everyone else in the village had been raised by their spiritual parents, unlike me and Oscar.

I gave a quick wave and out the door I went.

"June! Whoo hoo!" the voice called from down the sidewalk. It was Isadora Solstice. She stood at the steps of Mystic Lights. Her lighting shop was a cover up for her crystal ball reading spiritual gift. It was where I had found Madame Torres. Or rather Madame Torres finally found me.

Something else I'd had no idea about. The spiritualist didn't have a say in their crystal ball, the crystal ball picked the spiritualist. Madame Torres had sat on the shelf in Mystic Lights for centuries like a big round snow globe until I walked in. That was when she came to life and only I could see her.

"We moved the meeting time up so be there in an hour." She pushed her long blond wavy hair behind her shoulder before wiping her hands down her black A-frame skirt with the red hearts all over it. Her black pointy-toed boots were laced up tight. "I picked my skirt for you." She winked her big blue eyes and smiled. "For love." She clasped her hands as a delightful sigh escaped her.

"I'll see you soon!" I hurried across the street where A Charming Cure was located. I only had an hour to talk to Faith before the meeting and I wanted to make sure she was prepared, plus get my Mr. Sandman Sprinkles.

I stopped just shy of the gate that opened in front of the shop and looked down the street. Whispering Falls was so magical. The village was carved in the side of the mountain. The moss covered cottage shops were nestled into the woods and each had the most beautiful entrances. All the shops had colorful awnings with the shop's name on it.

The sidewalks on both sides were dotted with carriage lights with gas flames. Each shop had a special gate that led up to the shop steps, making the special village even cozier than it already was. There was already a line out the door of The Gathering Grove, the tea shop in the village. Tourists knew that they could go there for a nice breakfast before the rest of the shops opened.

A calmness came over me. I was being silly about going away. I was sure everything was going to be fine and Oscar was right. I was just stressed about my first time being on a plane and first time at the beach.

I opened the gate to A Charming Cure and a big whiff of the purple wisteria vine tunneled around me before I walked up the steps to the shop.

I reached up and ran my hand over the wooden sign that hung off the front of my cottage shop. The words *A*

Charming Cure had replaced the *A Dose of Darla* sign after I moved here and accepted my spiritual gifts.

There were two shop windows and Faith was working in the right one. She was hanging beach balls from the ceiling. The ladder she was standing on teetered when I walked in.

"How on Earth did you get that?" I pointed to the four-foot tall sand castle made of real sand and reached to steady her.

"A little bit of magic." Faith's blue eyes sparkled. The teetering ladder didn't phase her. "Your honeymoon has inspired me. And I saw the new line of sunscreen you left in the back. Mortals love going on summer vacations and if they can get something from here, we need to jump on it."

"You are so smart." I took a moment to look at the shop. Tiered display tables dotted the shop's floor. Each table had a long red tablecloth that grazed the floor. Different sized and colored ornamental bottles sat displayed on each table.

When I had taken over the shop, I categorized the different potions for different ailments. I kept the big chalkboards that Darla had put on the wall with the daily specials. In fact, the chalkboard closest to the counter still had *A Dose of Darla* written on it in Darla's handwriting, something I couldn't erase.

Another thing I moved was the inventory. Darla had kept her inventory and ingredients in the back room. I had made a couple of open shelves behind the counter to display them. It was neat to see the different bottles and ingredients and made the shop feel more organic. I had turned the back room into a little sitting room and while I did put extra inventory in there, I mainly used it for a place to eat lunch or relax while working late.

Keeping the ingredients behind the counter was perfect for when a customer came in for something to help with what they thought ailed them, I would talk to them and immediately get a sense of what was really going on. My best seller was by far the antacids. Customers thought they had acid reflux or some other stomach ailment, when in fact the root of their issue was stress over money or heartache. It was then that I took the homeopathic bottle they had chosen from the sales floor and gave it a special touch to address what really ailed them. All of my customers returned because my homeopathic cures worked.

Sunscreen was going to be a big one this year along with all the weight loss potions. I had made one that helped with hunger, changed bad thoughts about body image, and boosted confidence. Faith was right. The quicker we sold it, the word would get out and we wouldn't be able to keep them in stock.

After Oscar and I had planned to go on a honeymoon and set the date, I knew I was going to need to make up potions for Faith to have on hand. I had stored them in the back room, leaving her with plenty of stock while I was gone.

"I have to go to the village council within the hour." On my way back to the counter, I tugged and smoothed my hands over the display tables' covers. It was very important to me to have a beautiful shop.

I stopped shy of the counter and looked at the framed photo of my parents, Darla and Otto Heal, hanging on the wall. They would've loved this shop. I knew they already loved Oscar because they showed up in Madame Torres while Mr. Prince Charming was walking me down the aisle. It was amazing.

My image reflected from the framed glass. My short black bobbed hair grazed my bare shoulders. My blunt bangs crossed my forehead in a perfect line. The white and blue striped bandeau top was new. I'd bought it from a shop in Locust Grove and paired it with white shorts and gladiator sandals. I was definitely ready for the beach.

"Are you okay?" Faith called out over her shoulder. A sand pail dangled from her long finger.

"I'm fine," I said and picked up the chalk for the chalkboard. "I need to write the daily specials." Quickly and in fancy cursive, I wrote the sunscreen specials on the board. "Tomorrow we can keep the same special, but change it to the weight loss special in a couple of days."

I took a step back and looked at the board. The smells of cinnamon, sage, dill and thyme swirled around my head. I smiled and took another look around.

I walked behind the counter to get a good look at the ingredients on the shelf, and nearly jumped of my skin when Mr. Prince Charming leaped up on the counter next to me.

Rowl. He barely opened his mouth. He dropped something and nudged it with his nose. I gulped after seeing the spiral-shaped charm he'd pushed toward me. Fear, stark and sheer ripped through me when the memory of the orange spiral from my nightmare jolted my insides.

"You don't look fine. In fact," Faith glided toward me, "you look worse than when I asked you."

I put my hand on the counter over the charm, hoping she didn't see it. I raked it into my palm and put it in my front pocket. There was no way I wasn't going on this honeymoon and there was no need to alarm anyone that Mr. Prince Charming had given me another charm.

"I'm fine." A nervous laugh escaped me. "I think I'm just nervous about leaving the shop and home."

"It's all good. I've got this." She pointed to herself, then at me. "You need to go enjoy that hunk of yours."

My mind wasn't wrapped around that hunk of mine; my mind was wrapped around the spiral charm. Mr. Prince Charming had been giving me protection charms since he showed up on my tenth birthday. The first one was a small turtle and anytime he felt I was in danger or going to be in danger, a new charm showed up.

I ran my hand over my wrist and curled my fingers around my charm bracelet. What if Mr. Prince Charming was trying to tell me something about my nightmares? Or what if Madame Torres was right about me having to take him with us?

I looked back at the shelf of ingredients and contemplated my options. I could make my Mr. Sandman Sprinkles and take them on my honeymoon just in case I needed it or just take my chances. My thought processes lasted all of a second, at the most, and I reached for the Aconite, the first ingredient for my potion.

I flipped on my cauldron and measured out 30 c of the Aconite, dumping it into the cauldron. I mixed in 6c Kali phos, 6c Nat suph, 3x passiflora and stirred it slowly. The liquid curled and bubbled, nearly flowing over the top of the hot cauldron. The frothy mix puffed a couple of smoke signals in the air. The smoke bubbles popped, sending the smell of fresh ocean salt air into the open space.

My cures took on the favorite smells of the person it was intended for making it even more appealing for the recipient. In this case, I was the patient of my own cure.

"You better get going," Faith called out and nodded to the clock on the wall. "You have to get up to The Gathering Rock."

The Gathering Rock was a communal space where we held our village rituals and village meetings. It was a sacred place. It was my job to smudge the area clean of any evil.

The Mr. Sandman Sprinkles rolled and roared inside the cauldron until it came to an abrupt stop. I ran my finger along the empty bottles on the shelf, knowing the bottle that was meant for this potion would glow as soon as my finger touched it. A small, white, milk glass bottle with a simple cork top lit up.

"Perfect," I whispered, grabbing the bottle. I took the cork off and held it over the cauldron allowing the potion to magically transfer from the cauldron to the bottle. It was a phenomenon that I didn't bother trying to explain or understand, it was just accepted like my spiritual gift.

The smudge ceremony bag caught my attention when I grabbed a rag under the counter to wipe the cauldron. Happily, I smacked my hands together. Faith jumped.

"I'm so sorry." I grabbed my smudge bag. All of my stuff for the trip needed to be smudged. I also grabbed a bottle with a generic potion in it. It would help me feel better and help keep me safe along with the charms. My intuition that I relied on was going to be on high alert. The generic potion would be good to take on my trip as a base to any potion I might really need to make.

"Wait." Faith stepped in front of me when I walked out from behind the counter with my Mr. Sandman Sprinkles bottle and smudge bag. "You aren't supposed to take any potions or witchy things on vacation. Orders of Officer Park."

"I'm going to take this to the meeting," I lied. If I told her the truth, she would've told Oscar I was smudging our house and luggage. I had promised him no potions, no spiritual stuff, just me and him on the honeymoon.

I couldn't help it if I had an obligation to my spiritual side. Even if I couldn't put it aside for a week.

Faith gave me the stink eye. She closed her eyes. She sucked in a deep breath in her nose and released it in a slow steady exhale out of her mouth. Her onyx eyes opened.

"I don't hear anything." She had tapped into her spiritual gift of Clairaudience.

"Or the fact that you just broke the law." I referred to one of the by-laws of the village. Spiritualists cannot read another spiritualist. The second by-law was that if you owned a shop in Whispering Falls, you had to live in Whispering Falls.

"Pish posh." She flailed a limp hand in the air before I grabbed my black cross-body bag and flung it across me. "Like no one else does."

She was right. Even though it was a law, it was unspoken that we did dabble in reading each other. Out of curiosity and protection of our kind.

"Now go." She pointed to the door.

Mr. Prince Charming jumped off the counter. His long white tail dragged along the floor as he waited patiently for me.

"And I don't want to see you in here again until you get back!" she shouted before I shut the door behind me.

I ran my hand down into my pocket and felt the charm. I looked down at Mr. Prince Charming.

"What on Earth does this mean?" I asked him, hoping he'd just open that little mouth of pointy teeth and tell me. He didn't. He darted down the steps, out the gate and between A Charming Cure and A Cleansing Spirit Spa.

"Hi-do, June," Chandra Shango waved from the stoop of her pink cottage shop's door. She owned the spa where she did nails, hair, and massages. She was a palm reader and the spa was the perfect cover. She gave out advice like candy to her clients. They loved her. She was always booked. "Are you getting excited to find out your honeymoon destination?"

"Wanna give me a hint?" I elbowed her as we met in between our shops. "Hawaii?" I did a hula dance to each side. "Or Jamaica Man?" I asked in my best Rastafarian accent, which was not too good mixed into my southern, hick accent.

She wagged her blue painted fingernails with the little gold star in my face. She had on a blue cloak with yellow stars all over it. Her yellow turban had a blue jewel in the middle to match the cloak. "You know I can't tell you, but you are going to love it. More relaxing then any old massage."

We talked about this and that on our way up the hill to The Gathering Rock. She told me about her new adventure in acupuncture. I wasn't sure I'd let her do that to me. I'd seen her go off track and I didn't want to be a pin cushion.

The Gathering Rock was exactly what it was named after, a big, gigantic rock that was in front of a clearing that served as a communal area. The village council already had chairs set up in front of the rock that was believed in the spiritual world to have powers in itself. Hovering over the rock with long black cloaks dangling down from the air, legs crossed and black hats pointing to the sky were the Order Of Elders. The Marys to be exact—Mary Lynn, Mary Ellen, and Mary Sue. They were retired village presidents of other spiritual communities and they only came around when there was a problem, like when I was accused of killing someone, which I didn't do.

My insides curled. I ran my hand over my pocket and felt the charm. Did they know what Mr. Prince Charming had given me?

"What are they doing here?" I whispered to Chandra.

"They are nosy." She tapped her nose. "Always got to be in everyone's business."

"Hi." Oscar walked over to us and bent down to kiss me. His lips were warm and soft. A calmness spread over me like wildfire. "I can't wait to get away with you." His eyes slid over to Mr. Prince Charming.

Mary Ellen had released her legs and floated down to the ground. She landed on her leopard-print boots. She bent down and picked up the ornery cat and stroked him. He purred so loud that you could hear him over the murmur of the council as they got ready to give us our honeymoon location.

Everyone's eyes were on me, and my intuition kicked in. My mind and body flooded with the spiritual rights of the smudging ceremony. I walked up to The Gathering Rock and took the smudging kit out of my bag. The sage stick was filled with cleansing ingredients such as sagebrush, sage, sweetgrass, lavender, cedar, mugwort, juniper, yerba santa, and rosemary, each used for a different purpose. Most of them were used for cleansing, clearing negative, encouraging awareness, purifying and healing. I was looking more to the cedar's component of deeply clearing negative emotions and replacing with positive energy to surround me and Oscar on our honeymoon to help negate the nightmares.

Once I lit the stick, everyone closed their eyes and bowed their heads. I walked around the circle of spiritualists and took a handful of the sage smoke and blew it toward each one of their hearts as I walked past each spiritualist. As each person took a deep breath to allow the healing smoke to fill their lungs, I waved the long feather to deepen their awareness of the healing power and whispered, "Breathe in positivity, courage and love."

The chants that came out of me were not something I had come up with. The chants would come out of my mouth on their own as I went deeper and deeper into my intuitive spiritual gift. This particular chant seemed to be appropriate since the council was here to give me and Oscar our destination.

"And now we call on our ancestors and all the animals of the spiritual world to carry our love and light to the rest of the world in order of protection, healing and love," my voice lifted into the air as I waved the smudge stick around in the middle of the group allowing the animals with wings to fly into the smoke and carry the messages from our spiritual world.

The feathered friends chirped and squawked before flying off into a deafening silence. Once the silence blanketed us, instinctively we all opened our eyes and moved to our rightful places in the council meeting area.

"Order! Order!" Petunia Shrubwood called, smacking the gavel a little too loudly for baby Orin who cried out from the kangaroo pouch hanging down her front. She was the Village President and all too happy to be in her position. She was an animal whisperer and owned Glorybee Pet Shop. She and Gerald Regiula were married and had baby Orin. "I'm so sorry baby boy," she whispered to Orin.

Gerald rushed over and grabbed Orin from the pouch to console him. He took the top hat off his head and fanned the baby. Orin loved the breeze and cooed with happiness.

The village council consisted of Gerald, Petunia, Isadora and Chandra.

"I'd like to welcome everyone to our special session today as we discuss the honeymoon destination for June Heal and Oscar Park." Petunia motioned for us to come in front of the council.

We stood next to each other holding hands. He squeezed mine and looked down at me. The love and compassion in his eyes always amazed me. It's hard to believe that I was married to my childhood best friend. He knew that Darla never gave me sweet treats and so would knock on my window in the middle of the night with a box of Ding Dongs. I knew then that I loved him. It wasn't until we were grown and living in Whispering Falls did we give in to our attraction and the chemistry between us.

"The Order Of Elders is here to reiterate that there must be no magic performed outside of Whispering Falls." Petunia looked back at the Elders. All of them nodded in agreement. "We know that Oscar understands, but we need to know from you, June Heal, that you understand the by-laws since it seems to be you that breaks them the most and gets herself in trouble."

My jaw dropped, my eyes lowered. I couldn't believe Petunia would say that to me. Nervously she looked away and bit her bottom lip.

"I get it," I said in a flat tone. "Ouch." I jerked my hand away from Oscar when he squeezed it a little too hard.

"Then we have picked your destination." Petunia nodded to Isadora.

"We've picked the small island in the Caribbean, Tulip Island." Petunia lifted the large crystal ball in the air, waving her hand over it. "Tulip Island is a very small American island that only accommodates a few tourists at one time. This will help you keep a low profile and help stay out of trouble."

"Tulip Island?" Oscar stepped up. "I really wanted to go to Jamaica."

"I put down Hawaii." My confusion swirled around me.

"I'm sorry," Petunia couldn't even look at me. "Hawaii has the tiki legend and a spiritual community we'd like not to mingle with." She sucked in a deep breath through her nose. "And Jamaica has voodoo that we'd like to keep at a distance."

"It is certainly out of the question, with your wife's history, that we send you just anywhere in the world when we have to keep an eye on her." Elder Mary Sue pointed a finger at me. Her deep, brash voice boomed, "If you do not accept Tulip Island, you can honeymoon on top of the hill in your cottage."

"No, ma'am." Oscar stepped back in line. "We are more than happy to go to Tulip Island." He nudged me. "Right, honey?"

Mary Ellen put a squirming Mr. Prince Charming down on the ground. He ran over and reared up on his hind legs, batting his front paws on my pocket where I had put the charm.

"What is wrong with your familiar?" Elder Mary Lynn squeaked from the air. She stroked her fox stole that was around her neck.

"Oh no," Oscar groaned from under his breath.

Chapter Two

"Why didn't you tell me about the new charm?" Oscar stalked after me on our way back to the cottage. "You and I both know that, that, that," he spat and stuttered before he stumbled over his own feet because he was so mad at Mr. Prince Charming.

"He gave it to me right before the meeting." I stalked beside him.

"Then you should've told me before the meeting." He wasn't getting it.

"I didn't have time, Oscar." My words were bitter and to the point. "I had a smudge to do and not only that, but this was something that you and I should discuss in private. If the council knew about the charm, they wouldn't let us go to Tulip Island, wherever that is."

The fact that they said they had to watch me angered me more than thinking I needed some protection.

"What am I supposed to do, Oscar?" I asked using his name which meant only one thing. . .I was mad. And at him. "He is my familiar. I can't control what he sees and knows. I don't even know how he knows it. All I know is that every single time he's given me a charm it has been for protection."

"Did this have anything to do with your dream?" he asked calmly.

I shrugged and turned around to head back to the cottage, putting distance between us. "You know and I know that I don't remember all of the dreams. All I know is that there was a man drowning."

"Fine!" he yelled after me because I was tired of listening to his lecture and wanted to get out of there as fast as possible. "We aren't going to the island."

"Oh yes we are!" I yelled back, my hands fisted at my side.

"June!" he yelled louder than I'd ever heard him yell. There was anger in his voice that made me pause. He caught up with me and put his arm around me. "We are not going. I will not have you anywhere near water if this is the case. We are going for relaxation, not work."

"Then I will just go by myself." I knew I sounded like a baby. But in my head I had reasoned with myself that if I didn't hang around anyone else on the tiny island but Oscar, then we would be fine. All fine. I wouldn't see a man. I wouldn't see the spiral. All fine.

"I'm not going to work. I'm going to relax with some books that Ophelia has waiting for me at Ever After Books. While you work on your tan, I will sit happily under the umbrella and read." I think I even made myself believe my own words. "If what Isadora says is true and the island is much smaller than even Whispering Falls," I gestured down the hill over our village as we stood on the front porch, "then we won't run into anyone."

He looked at me for a moment too long and let out a deep sigh. He reached around me and opened the door to the cottage.

"We have a day to think about it." We stepped inside. "I need to do some investigating about the possibilities of this happening. And I hate to even say it, but if Mr. Prince Charming and Madame Torres turn up something else in the next twenty-four hours that means you are going to be in the middle of some murder investigation, then we won't be going."

"Fine." I crossed my arms in front of me, my fingers crossed underneath the fold.

"Fine." He walked around me and back to the bedroom. "I'm going to get my clothes together for the trip and I suggest you do the same."

My lip curled and I admit I was pouting. But there was no way I wasn't going to go on this honeymoon. Charm or not. Oscar had been looking forward to this for so long that even a little nightmare wasn't going to stop me.

I ran my hand down into the front pocket of my shorts and pulled the charm out. I knew what I needed to do next. Exactly what I did every time one of these charms was dropped in front of me. Go see Bella Van Lou, owner of Bella's Baubles and the shop where Mr. Prince Charming conveniently stole the charms from.

"I'm going to pick up those books," I called from the family room back toward the bedroom, leaving out the fact I was going to go see Bella first.

"Okay. Let Colton know that I'm going to soak up some sun for him if you see him." Oscar joked about Ophelia's boyfriend, Colton Lance, the co-sheriff with Oscar in Whispering Falls.

I grabbed my bag off the hook and headed out the door and down the hill. The street was packed with tourists and I was happy to notice customers were in A Charming Cure. I would stop by to make sure Faith was doing all right after I got my books, but first things was first.

Bella's Baubles was the only jewelry store in Whispering Falls and was like the rest, a cover for Bella's spiritual gift. She was an astrologer and she was able to read gemstones. The cream cottage style shop with the pink wood door was just as charming as Bella herself. It was a perfect time to visit because the sun was coming up perfectly over the mountains and shining down on the pink door where there were all sorts of gems embedded making a rainbow of crystals dart all over town. It was truly beautiful.

Every time I read the store's hours painted on the door, I smiled. Open Morning to Night. She was as clever as she was amazing. When I stepped through the door, Mr. Prince Charming darted through my legs and jumped on the jewelry display case where Bella was showing a customer a square-shaped ruby. But only when the bell dinged above the door announcing my arrival did she look up.

"Good morning, June." She smiled exposing the space between her two front teeth and the balled-up cheeks. "I was expecting you." She straightened up, her long blond hair cascaded down her five-foot-two-inch frame. She ran her slender hand down Mr. Prince Charming, white strands of fur flying with each stroke. "I'll be with you in a moment."

"I'm in no hurry." I browsed around the shop and listened to her talk her customer into buying the ruby stone instead of the sapphire the man insisted on buying his wife as a gift because she'd just gotten a promotion.

"She loves the blue tones." He shook his head.

"Yes, but your wife is one of character and strength. Not only is the ruby the most precious of gems, but it will propel her to leadership of the company." Bella casually pushed the stone toward him and retracted the sapphire that lay on the black display cloth. "She does want to be the CEO of the company, am I right?"

Bella was able to tap into the man's wife through him and she knew exactly what his wife needed to go forward in her success. Rarely did one of Bella's customers walk out of the jewelry shop with what they had come in to buy. And they all were returning customers.

"The sapphire is a meditation of sorts. Easy. And we don't want her to be meditating on the job do we?" Bella went in for the kill. "I'll tell you what." She picked up the square ruby and placed it in the palm of his hand. She curled his fist with hers and said, "If your wife doesn't see movement toward another new role in the company that has to do with making her CEO faster than anticipated, you come back and see me. Not only will I give your money back, but you can keep the ruby and I will give you the sapphire."

"Can I get that in writing?" the man asked in a leery voice.

"All done." Bella reached under the display and pulled out a piece of paper.

The man stood with his mouth opened, stunned. After the transaction and money was exchanged, the man left happy.

"I do love when they come back." She drummed her fingers together and watched out the window at the man getting into his car. She pushed back her hair, bringing it into the grip of her hand and pulling it around her shoulder, letting it rest down the front of her. She turned to me. "Now. I guess you are here about a little spiral charm." She stuck her hand out in front of her palm up.

I took the charm and my bracelet and put them in her open palm. She curled them into her fist, closed her eyes and took a deep breath.

"Courage, bravery, and awareness." Her words were slow and static. "Aware of your surroundings."

She opened her eyes and smiled.

"So what does that mean?" I asked. "Specifically to my trip."

"This is a nice charm he's picked this time." Bella rubbed down Mr. Prince Charming and I swear he smiled with pride underneath the loud purr. "There are several meanings to the charm, but for you and your trip, it only means that you need to be aware of your surroundings."

"That's it?" I asked. "Nothing evil, bad?" I shook my head.

"Just be aware. Keep your eyes open and awake." Her cryptic language stuck me in my gut. There had to be more than just being aware, but I had to take her for her word. I couldn't ask her to give me a full reading because of the by-laws, but I sure wished she would. I had to take the meaning of the charm and somehow relate it to my life at that moment.

"Which I guess would make sense because we are going to a tropical island with only a few people on it." I smiled, brushing off any notions about a bad honeymoon. Now I felt like I should run back to the cottage and hug Oscar.

"Good." She clapped her hands together in delight. The bell dinged over the door and a new customer walked in. "Have a wonderful time and take plenty of pictures."

"Pictures." I groaned. I'd forgotten to get my camera from the house in Locust Grove. "I've got to go and get some books Ophelia has picked out for my trip."

"Come back after and I'll have this ready for you." She patted the bundle of charms and set them on the counter. She was always so good about putting the new charm on and getting it back on my wrist as soon as possible.

I waved and let her take care of the next customer. I crossed the street and waved at Raven through the glass window of Wicked Good. She had a line out the door. It was so nice to see the village doing so well. It hit me right then. I was probably feeling all weird because I had never left Whispering Falls for a long period of time as a spiritualist. I had to wonder what it was going to be like as a witch in a community of only mortals for a full week.

"June," Isadora, Izzy for short, waved from the door of her shop. She wore a ring on her middle finger. It was in the shape of a curled up cat. She brought me out of my thoughts. "I know the remote island wasn't what Oscar and you requested, but we felt it was in your best interest. And now that Oscar has decided that he would like Madame Torres to accompany you, it tells me that he is also glad we are sending you there."

"He what?" I threw open the gate to her shop and walked up the steps. Mr. Prince Charming came out of nowhere and started to do his signature figure eight around my ankles. "He came to you?"

"Yes, he just left." She lifted her arm. I followed the length of it down to where she was pointing, just in time to see Oscar turn behind A Charming Cure. "Didn't he tell you?" Her question was more judgmental than questioning.

My silence was enough of an answer. He didn't say a word to me about Madame Torres. He said he was packing.

"I saw you come out of Bella's so I'm assuming Mr. Prince Charming gave you a charm?" She drew her eyes down to the ground and watched as he curled his long white tail around my leg.

"He did. A spiral charm and I didn't think anything of it as real protection until Oscar came here. He is the one who assured me that everything was going to be okay and my nightmare was silly." I was starting to guess that my theory my nightmare was caused by the stress of me being gone was wrong. Izzy strolled up next to me. I said, "He said that I was stressed because I was going to the beach for the first time and riding in a plane for the first time." Dumb me.

"He said that you had a nightmare and told him you didn't want to go on the honeymoon. So to ease your fear of anything happening, I felt it best that Madame Torres ride along in your suitcase." Izzy curled her arm around my shoulder.

Rowl! Mr. Prince Charming batted the air and ran off.

"Yeah, he's not going to stand for that." My brows lifted. "I'm guessing he can't go?"

"We would have to get special clearance from the mortals and that is just something I don't feel is necessary." I heard the words that were coming from her mouth, but my thoughts were right back at the nightmare. "A lot of islands require the animal be quarantined so they don't bring unwanted diseases onto the island. Since you are only going to be gone a week, I figured you can use Madame Torres to not only ask how things are going here, but also keep an eye out for things there."

"Well, let's hope so," I said blankly. "I've got to go see Ophelia. She's got some books waiting for me to take and read." I paused. "If I'm not working on figuring out my nightmare while on the island."

"You will be fine." Izzy pish-poshed me and tucked her hands in the pockets of her skirt.

I just couldn't believe that Oscar would get clearance for me to take Madame Torres. That only meant one thing to me, that my dream and my fears had him on high alert. Before he was adamant about it being just me and him. Alone at last. Well, Mr. Prince Charming might not be able to come, but a bunch of my potions and my Magical Cures Book were definitely fitting in my suitcase. I glanced over at my shop. It looked full so going in to hide some potions in my purse was going to have to wait until there weren't so many eyes around.

"Hi, June." Ophelia Biblio was sitting on the floor in the children's section with the small kids gathered around her. "Your books are on the counter." She continued reading the book to the children.

Her soft voice drew me in and I quietly sat for a few minutes and enjoyed her reading the story and watched one little girl in particular twirling a strand of Ophelia's curly honey hair around her finger as she was mesmerized by Ophelia's reading. I got up when I noticed she had a stack of children's books next to her and the sign behind her said that story time was an hour long and it had just begun.

I looked through the books she had stacked for me on the counter. There were a couple romance books that looked steamy enough for a honeymoon, a memoir about one of our spiritual guides, a map of Tulip Island, and a myths and legends book of the island. She gave me a thumbs-up when I glanced back at her, curious about the island books. I took them anyway so I wouldn't hurt her feelings and made a mental note to leave them at home. I wasn't going to spend my honeymoon exploring myths and legends of an island. At least I didn't think so.

Chapter Three

"Did you get any interesting books?" Oscar asked when I walked through the front door of our cottage. He was sitting on the couch with Mr. Prince Charming. The two were making nice. Well, at least Mr. Prince Charming was. There was no doubt in my mind he knew that Oscar was the one he was going to have to suck up to if he wanted to be included on the trip.

"She gave me some good smutty ones." I showed him the covers. "I guess I have to read them," my words dripped with sarcasm. "But these." I held up the two books about the island. "These can stay home."

"Let me see." He wiggled his fingers toward me. I leaned forward to hand him the books, but he grabbed me instead, pulling me in for a nice long and soft kiss. "I can't wait to spend time with you on the beach."

"Me and Madame Torres?" I asked, still wrapped up in his arms. Mr. Prince Charming climbed up on my arm as though he were on a tightrope and kneaded me.

"Not you." Oscar looked at the cat. "You stay here and hold down the fort."

Rowl. Mr. Prince Charming jumped down but not without digging his claws in my skin.

"Ouch!" I jerked my arm up and looked at the four little blood spots. "He is not happy and neither am I. Why did you go behind my back about Madame Torres?"

"It wasn't behind your back. I wanted clearance from the council before I suggested it to you. She will make you feel better and not worried while we are gone." He sat up and raked his hands through his hair before he leaned up on the edge of the couch and put his hands between his legs. "She can show you the shop so you won't be calling Faith all the time and if something strange does happen, she'll be there for whatever it is she does as your familiar. Mr. Prince Charming would have to go through customs and red tape. She just looks like a snow globe knick-knack thingy."

"I'm not a knick-knack." A bright light shined from the bedroom and down the hall.

"You shouldn't have said that." I rolled my eyes. "But when you put it that way, it does make sense."

"Let me make it up to you." He pulled me back into his arms. There was no place that I ever felt safer. "I've made a reservation for two at the Treesort for dinner."

"You did?" I asked and stared into his big blue eyes. I watched his strong jaw as he spoke.

"I did." He pushed me to stand. "Go get ready and we can go. I'm starving."

"But it's not dinner time." I looked at the clock in the kitchen. We usually didn't eat dinner in the early afternoon, but then again we usually weren't home then either.

"It's vacation time." A wicked grin passed over his lips before he smacked me on the hiney.

"I might get used to honeymoon time." I giggled and scurried down the hall.

Madame Torres's face was bobbling up and down in the glass globe. Her eyes narrowed and her lips pursed. She was not happy.

"If you think that you are going to get me on a plane. . ." Her eyes rolled side-to-side. "Then you have another thing coming."

"Why is it that when I really need you, you want to give me a hard time?" I asked a simple question. It was true. She was always so mad, but she did always come to my rescue.

"Take the furball." Her eyes shifted to the bed where Mr. Prince Charming had curled up on Oscar's pillow. Oscar would die if he saw Mr. Prince Charming there. He was okay with him on the bed, but not on his pillow.

"You were the chosen one." I decided a little flattery might get me somewhere.

"Unchoose me." Her head spun around and around until the inside of the ball went black. It was her way of having a crystal ball hissy fit. She was good at it.

"Almost ready?" Oscar stuck his head in. "Get that cat off my pillow! Gross!"

Mr. Prince Charming lifted his head, twitched his lip and laid it back down.

"Go on," I suggested. "You move him."

Oscar huffed down the hall knowing good and well he better leave the cat there or there would be consequences before, during and after we were at dinner.

"Play nice," I warned my familiars as I quickly slipped on a little strappy black dress. It wasn't like the Treesort restaurant was five-star or anything, but it was a date with Oscar and those were few and far between.

The Full Moon Treesort was the only bed and breakfast in town. It was something to behold. Amethyst Plum was the owner and proprietor of the Treesort and she'd had a brilliant idea. The resort lodge and the rooms are built in the forest trees beyond The Gathering Rock and my little cottage. The main lodge was the most spectacular place you'd ever see and the rooms were in separate trees around the property. They were so romantic and Amethyst had given a free stay to me and Oscar as a wedding present. And it couldn't be more fitting that we have dinner at Full Moon since Amethyst's spiritual gift is Onerirocriticy, dream interpretation. It couldn't be more perfect timing.

"Sonny was having a hard time finding someone to take my shift while I'm gone." Oscar made small talk as we walked into the woods, hand-in-hand as he referred to his boss at the police station in Locust Grove.

Mr. Prince Charming couldn't stand being left home; he was suddenly beside us leading the way as his tail darted up and down.

"He said that everyone is trying to go on vacation." He helped me over a log that had fallen. "I need to tell Colton to send someone out here and clear the trail for the tourists."

Oscar's thoughts were all over the place and so was the conversation, as though he was nervous.

"And you say that I have a hard time turning off work." I made note. I understand him though, because it was not only my work, it'd become my way of life just as his has. "We are on vacation. No work talk."

A group of fireflies danced the trail in front of us, lighting up the path that had been darkened by the canopy of the full leaves of the tree branches overhead.

"You kids are out early." I noted as they buzzed about. The souls of teenagers that went to the great beyond came back in the form of fireflies. Just like teenagers, they loved to flutter around all night and sleep all day. "Go on and tell Petunia I'm doing fine."

No doubt they were there to check up on me for Petunia. I was sure she wanted them to make sure I was okay with the village council's ruling earlier today about Tulip Island. After all, we were friends and we would never want anything to come between us.

"Just think." Oscar stopped when the path ended and the Full Moon Treesort was in front of us. "We got married right there underneath the stars."

"We did." I looked up at the massive double-decker A-frame resort that was mostly windows. There was a large staircase that led up to the Treesort lodge and the first step was where we got married in front of all our friends and family. It had truly been an amazing night.

Step by step we climbed to the top and Mr. Prince Charming was already inside doing what he did best. Begging for some of Amethyst's good food. The aroma of freshly baked bread floated on the late afternoon wind, leaving us with watering mouths. Inside the main room of the resort there were couches filled with the resort's clients. There was a big stone fireplace in the center of the room that served as a wall between the kitchen and the gathering space. The kitchen had a long counter with stools so some of Amethyst's clients could sit there and chit-chat with her while she prepared meals. Or they could sit at one of the private dining tables.

Oscar and I waved to her.

"Our favorite Whispering Falls couple." Amethyst untied the apron from around her waist and neck, setting it aside as she hurried over to greet us with a peck on the cheek. "I've got your table ready." She batted her long lashes under her thick brows. Her dark eyes danced as she tugged her black fishtail braid around her shoulder.

"Oh. Fancy." I smiled. "I thought we were going to sit at the counter."

"Not tonight." She had a singularly sweet smile. She motioned for us to follow her.

We followed her and I couldn't help but notice she looked much thinner in her black pencil pants and the sleeveless green blouse. Her arms were thinner than I recalled.

"How are you doing?" I asked, a concern in my tone.

"I'm all right. A little stressed with such little help." She opened the door to the outside balcony where there was a café table for two, a single white rose in a white milk vase with two lit tapered candles on each side. There were two place settings along with a bottle of wine next to the table in a chiller. "But that is how it is during the busy season."

"Oh you shouldn't have said that." Oscar gave me the eye because in the beginning when he wanted to take the honeymoon, I knew it was going to be the busy season, but I went along with it since I had Faith.

"I'm sorry." There was an empathetic look on her face as she pulled out my chair and offered me to sit.

"It's all good." I shook my head and tucked a strand of hair behind my ear. "When I get back, if there is anything I can do, you let me know."

"I will do that. Now, I've taken the liberty to prepare a special dinner for the two of you using some of your aunt Eloise's fresh vegetables from the garden." She poured some wine in each flute. "Enjoy the view."

We all took a moment to look out over the balcony and appreciate the colorful treetops and view of Whispering Falls in the distance. Pops of colorful flowers dotted Amethyst's garden off the to the right of the resort. The fragrance of the flowers filled all of the universe.

"That was nice of Eloise to send fresh vegetables." I picked up my glass and took a sip.

"I had asked her to send some of your favorites. I really want the honeymoon to be special. Me and you." He reached over and put his hands on mine. "We deserve this."

"Yes you do." The familiar voice of my great aunt Helena chimed over my shoulder. "You deserve a lot of things in life, but that doesn't happen very often." She tapped me on the shoulder. "We need to talk. Privately."

She was good at being the bearer of bad news and was a pessimist regarding most situations.

Oscar's head tilted a little to the right, his brows hooded and his mouth slightly opened. It was not a good time to protest Aunt Helena. She didn't live in Whispering Falls. She was the Dean of Hidden Halls, A Spiritualist University where most of the spiritualists I knew had gone to school. I had even taken a few classes myself when I had learned of my gift. That was where I'd met Faith and Raven, though I'd like to forget about that since we didn't hit it off right away.

Regardless, I got up and gave Oscar the "it will only be a minute" look even though we both knew she would take longer than that.

She swept her long black cloak around her body. There was a glimpse of the toe of her red pointy boots. She twirled to face the opening of the lodge and tapped her way inside with me following behind her. Once inside, she passed the kitchen and went straight past the fireplace and out the door.

"Where are we going?" I asked as she trotted down the front steps of the Treesort and into the woods. She didn't respond. She simply kept going until we were deep into the woods and the darkness settled in quicker than normal. I glanced around to see if any fireflies were going to light my way, but we were alone. All alone.

The moon appeared above and the leaves on the tree gave a slight whisper as the night breeze drifted around causing them to dance in the moonlight and create a dance floor on the earth. Aunt Helena threw the cloak from around her and let it sweep behind her. Three owls flew down from the trees and surrounded her, hooting and flapping their wings.

Aunt Helena's long red hair dragged down her back as her head floated backward and her arms lifted to the side.

There was some sort of spell going on that I was not aware of. In fact, I'd never seen many of her spells or her at work. She was magical in many ways and she let young spiritualists learn on their own and perfect their gift. Even though I am her niece, I had no insight to what she was really capable of.

She pulled her head up and opened her eyes. They shot sparks of emerald colored streams as if her eye color was bleeding out. Her lips opened and she chanted, "By the light of the owl moon on this summer night, I call thee to give she your might, by the power of the three, I conjure thee to protect she with these."

Aunt Helena clapped her hands and held her fingers out to each owl. One by one, they pecked her with their beaks, each drawing blood from a different finger.

"Surround thee, surround thee," she chanted and moved from the circle of the owls to circle me. She clapped up my body and down my body before going around my body. "Mote it be. Mote it be!"

She dropped to the ground just as the owls floated up through the trees and the silence wrapped around us like a blanket.

"Aunt Helena, what was that?" My voice pierced the dark and it almost hurt my ears. I gulped when she didn't move. A chill ran up my legs, along my core, and across my shoulders down to the tips of my fingers.

I extended my hand to touch her and a spark of electricity shot through my veins and out the tip of my finger hitting Aunt Helena.

Her body shot her up in the air. Her limbs limp, her head flailed backward, her hair dangling and eyes closed, she spoke, "Mote it be."

"Mote it be," the words came out of my mouth as if I had no control.

Aunt Helena floated down and solidly landed on her feet. She brushed her hands together and looked at me.

"Now that that is over," she said and walked past me. "You can go back to dinner with Oscar but do not breathe a word of this to anyone."

"I wouldn't even know what to tell them if I did." I stalked behind her. "So are you going to tell me what that was and why you wanted me to see it?"

"I transferred one of my gifts to you." She stopped and twirled around. Her cloak wrapped around her. "Now you can go on your honeymoon and I can be of sound mind."

"What?" I shook my head. "What power? Sound mind? Are you worried?" I shot questions at her like they were horses jumping out of the starting gate.

"Those." She pointed the long red fingernail of her pointer finger toward my hands. "I gave you my gift of using your fingers and your thoughts as you see fit. You want a drink. Voila." She snapped her fingers, nothing appeared. She grinned. "Now you try."

I thought of the glass of wine back at the lodge sitting on the table where my husband was waiting for me to return and snapped my fingers. It appeared in my hand.

"Oh my," I gasped. "This is interesting."

"And you can use it for not so great moments like if you were in trouble and needed something not accessible to you. Like a potion." Her eyes drew down her nose and her lips curled up. "But don't let anyone see you use it."

She seemed pleased but it only alarmed me. Actually, it scared me a little.

"So you think I'm going to need this special power?" I gulped and thought about my bracelet that Bella had as I wrapped my hand around my wrist. The spiral charm literally spiraled around my brain—it actually gave me an instant headache. I narrowed my eyes.

"Tap your temple," Aunt Helena instructed me.

I lifted my hand and took a quick glance at my finger before I tapped the pad against my temple. Instantly the pressure in my head was gone.

"Anything." She laughed. "But only for the specific time you are gone. Then it reverts back to me."

"Wow," was all I could muster up. "If I'd known this, I'd have begged for some other gift," I said half joking.

"This is something between me and you." Aunt Helena walked closer to me, she whispered, "I do not agree with the council letting you be gone for a week without Mr. Prince Charming, so I felt I needed to protect you in my own way. This will be a good gift from me to you."

Literally as in gift.

"Thank you." I smiled. She was my only living blood relative and I was glad she was there. We walked back to the lodge and I told her about the charm and my nightmare. She agreed with Oscar that it could be something to do with my nerves and leaving the secure village since I hadn't gone on a vacation since we moved there. But she also agreed that it could be a vision like the other nightmares I'd had. I was going to go with the first guess she had and would use the finger spell gift only if I needed it for real protection.

"I'll leave you here." She placed both hands on either side of my deltoids and gave a light squeeze. "You have a wonderful time. I can't wait to see the photos."

"Photos." I hit the palm of my hand to my head, realizing I'd forgotten to go to my house in Locust Grove to retrieve my old camera. Suddenly I was holding a camera.

"It's a wonderful gift." Aunt Helena curled the edges of the cloak around her before she snapped her arm down to her side and in a plume of yellow smoke, she was gone.

Mr. Prince Charming caught me off guard when I looked down and he was there next to me.

"I guess I better go eat." I gestured him to follow me and strapped the camera over my shoulder.

The food was already on the table when I got back and the bottle of wine was almost empty.

Oscar's fingers drummed on top of the table and his other hand was curled around a wine glass. He brought the glass up to his lips and downed the last sip. His eyes focused on me. There was no spark, no sparkle or even a hint of happiness.

"I know." Immediately I began to apologize. "You know Aunt Helena." I gave a half smile and took the camera strap off my shoulder before I placed it on the table. "She wants to make sure we are going to be safe and sound. I'm sorry."

He reached over and grabbed the camera. "This is really nice." The smile that had always brought a sprinkle of joy in my soul appeared. "We need a good camera."

"Yeah." I bit my lip, my brows furrowed. I wasn't sure how I was going to explain the camera when Aunt Helena said I couldn't tell anyone about my new, if only part-time, gift.

"This is an actual gift your aunt has given us that we can use." He took the lens cover off and looked through the viewer. "I mean, like the crystal she gave us for the cottage porch as a wedding gift, what on Earth are we going to do with that?"

"Um. . ." I stuttered and pondered my options for about a split second. "Yes. I was thrilled she gave us the camera."

Technically I didn't lie. She did give us the camera by giving me the new gift.

"Now I don't have to go to Locust Grove and get one." I sucked in a deep breath and emptied the rest of the wine into my glass.

For a few minutes, Oscar and I sat in silence and enjoyed the amazing dinner Amethyst had prepared for us. By the time we finished our last bite, the sun had completely gone down over Whispering Falls and the wooded area was lit up by the fireflies. They darted about the branches and tree trunks leaving a little trail of sparkle behind them.

"Are you getting excited?" Oscar asked.

The discreet rattle of a pastry cart pulled up next to our table.

"I am." I tried my best to make it sound as convincing as possible even though the tug at my gut and Mr. Prince Charming's spiral charm told me to be careful.

To my delight, the cart was filled with real Ding Dongs.

"Don't tell Raven." Amethyst winked. A smile crawled to her lips and curled itself like a snake.

"Mums the word." I grabbed one and tore into it giving Oscar the other half before I devoured it.

"Are you ready? We have a big morning ahead of us and I still need to pack."

"Yes, ma'am," Oscar joked and stood up to help me out of my chair. He turned me toward him and placed both hands alongside my face. His gaze was as soft as a caress. "June, you make me the happiest man on the earth."

His lips met mine. He whispered, "Do you have time to do more than pack?"

Little did he realize that his kiss was more persuasive than he knew.

Chapter Four

"Who are you?" The salt water swished up against my shoulders. The man's diamond eyes stared at me. His coal black hair was slicked back. There was a mole on the side of his face. "Please tell me." I begged to know. I needed to know. "I can help you change your fate."

The thunderous sound overhead caught my attention. The sound of lapping water curled around the both of us as the sandy sea floor underneath me gave way. A wave behind the man's bobbing head was building.

"Tell me!" I begged before the wave plunged over him and me, taking us both under. An orange swirl dug deep beneath the water's surface, circling around the drowning man. He stretched his arm toward me and I reached. . .

I sat straight up in bed, gasping for air. Mr. Prince Charming's eyes glowed in the darkness of the bedroom. He pawed at me. The insides of Madame Torres swirled in a fit of orange rage, settling into a picture of the Magical Cures Book.

Meow, Mr. Prince Charming's lips moved, but nothing came out.

I peeled back the covers and eased myself out of bed so as not to wake Oscar. He would never approve of me getting up in the middle of the night to go to A Charming Cure to get the necessary items I needed to take with me.

I grabbed my clothes off the floor, where they had landed once Oscar and I had gotten home from all the food and wine drinking, and scurried out of the bedroom, getting dressed in the hall. Mr. Prince Charming was already waiting by the door. I grabbed my bag and my keys before I headed down the hill.

"Stop." I waved the fireflies away from my face and ran down the hill as fast as I could. There wasn't a lot of time to spare. Oscar might wake up and he wouldn't be happy if he did and I wasn't there.

All of the shops were dark. The gates glistened underneath the full moonlight. I stepped up on the sidewalk and took a few steps toward A Charming Cure; the Singing Nettles flowers in the flowerbox underneath the A Cleansing Spirit Spa's window hummed a sleepy tune.

"I'm so sorry," I apologized when I walked by and a few of them were yawning.

"June?" The voice appeared before the person stepped out of the shadow. "Are you okay?"

"Petunia." My heart thundered in my chest. Baby Orin was strapped in the Kangaroo pouch on the front of her. Lightly she bounced on the balls of her toes and patted his hiney. A bird's head popped in and out of the side of her messy up-do with each bounce. "You scared me."

I looked down at Orin and smiled. I ran a hand along his sleeping body.

"Orin was having a rough night, so we decided the Singing Nettles and full moon were just the trick he needed." She looked down at her baby with pride on her face. "Now, what about you?"

"I guess I needed the Singing Nettles too." I winked. I did love hearing them hum and sing in harmony. In fact, they were one of Darla's favorite flowers to look at even though she couldn't hear them since she wasn't a spiritualist. She knew they were special even without knowing their true beauty.

"Want to talk about it?" She took her comforting hand off Orin and placed it on me. "I don't know any woman who'd come out to the shop in the mid-morning hours before she left on a fabulous vacation unless something was wrong." Her eyes drew down with a curious brow lift. "And the teenagers told me you were a little restless earlier when you were going to dinner with Oscar at Full Moon Treesort." The teens flittered around and around, lighting our way over to the gate of my shop.

"Can't get nothing past those nosy kids." I joked and placed a hand on the gate before I opened it. I looked back but she wasn't following me. "You can come on in."

Mr. Prince Charming rushed in as soon as I opened the door. I flipped the lights on. A sense of calm swept over me as the shop lights lit up the magical bottles.

"Almost breath taking." Petunia looked around the room at the twinkling glass. "You do amazing work."

"Thank you." I walked back to the counter to retrieve the Magical Cures Book and noticed my charm bracelet was lying next to the register. Mr. Prince Charming jumped up and pawed the bracelet. I glanced up at Petunia. I couldn't tell if she was assessing the situation as a friend or as the Village President. "You might've picked where Oscar and I are going for our honeymoon, but it still won't keep us completely safe."

"How do you figure?" She pushed her hand up into her messy brown up-do and pulled a piece of catnip out of it along with a mouse toy. She tossed both onto the floor.

Mr. Prince Charming couldn't resist. He jumped down and batted the mouse before he sniffed the catnip and rolled all over it.

"I keep having a nightmare about water that I can only think to be the ocean. There was even a salty taste in my mouth." It wasn't like I was breaking any of the by-laws; I was sharing with her. Allowing her to give an opinion.

"You know as well as I do what happens when I have a nightmare."

She brought her hands up to her face and drummed the pads of her fingers together. "Yes." Her lips pursed. "Something bad happens—like a death."

"Exactly." I turned around and ran my finger down the shelf of glass bottles where I kept all of my ingredients for the potions and stopped at the Alder Bark. "This one will be good."

I grabbed the bottle and returned back to the counter where I disappeared behind the partition where I kept my cauldron. I flipped on the switch and opened the Alder Bark, sprinkling a few drops into the cauldron.

"Here." Petunia walked behind the partition and pulled a twig from her hair. "Blessed Thistle will help strengthen the potion and protect even more."

"Thank you." I smiled when I took it. "You are a good friend."

It was then that I knew I could confide in her as a friend tonight. I returned to the cauldron and stirred the bark with the thistle, letting them dissolve into each other before I retrieved the Magical Cures Book from underneath the counter.

The tattered journal would do its magic as soon as I touched it and would open up to the exact page I needed. The potion of extra protection called for Laurel Leaves, which made me pause because it was used for males in weddings and since Oscar and I had already said our I-do's, I wasn't clearly sure on what this was for, but I still grabbed the bottle off the shelf. Echinacea didn't surprise me since it was good for strengthening spells, but a pattern was emerging for me.

"There is a lot of strengthening in all of these ingredients." I chewed the corner of the inside of my lip and read through it again to make sure. Before I could even pick up the ladle to stir, the cauldron smoked with jade streaks running up in the air. The smell of sugar drifted out of the smoke, leaving a chemical taste in my mouth after it was inhaled through my nostrils. I circled my hand over the cauldron and let the elixir dance the way it had chosen, which was in the motion of waves of the ocean as if it knew my dream. Underneath my fingertips, the mixture fizzled, bubbled, and moved as the ingredients became one.

On the shelf beyond the partition were the empty glass bottles that spoke to me when they glowed. The simple crystal with the cork top shimmered and glistened, calling me to pick it. When I touched it, I knew the small electric charge that hit my fingertips had a mighty power and it was the right bottle for the potion I was going to take with me for extra protection—even if I was just being overly cautious.

"And." I looked over at Petunia, who was breast-feeding Orin. "I can't let Oscar know because I told him that I wouldn't do any sort of spell."

"June." Petunia's jaw dropped. "You cannot do that."

"He went to Izzy and talked to her about me taking Madame Torres, so he knows I'm worried." I held the bottle over the top of the cauldron and let the potion magically fill up the crystal bottle. "If he's worried, then I'm a tad bit worried."

"Maybe he's just being cautious." She brought Orin up to her shoulder and burped the sleeping baby. "He always falls asleep feeding, but he will be right back up in a minute." She tucked him back in the pouch. "I want you two to have a wonderful time."

"I'm sure we will." I picked up the bracelet and clasped it around my wrist. I grabbed the book and the potion and put them in my bag before I strapped it across me. "I better get going before Oscar wakes up and sees I'm gone."

I took one last look around the shop once Petunia stepped outside with Mr. Prince Charming. Everything looked like it was ready for Faith to take over for the time I was gone and I liked how the shop welcomed her. I flipped the lights off and locked it up tight before I darted down the front steps, out of the gate and up the hill to where I was happy to see Oscar still asleep.

Our suitcases were packed and unzipped on the floor of the family room. I took the items out of my bag and pushed the book and potions to the bottom of my suitcase, sticking all the clothes on top. I crept into the bedroom and snatched Madame Torres from the side table.

"What are you doing?" Her face floated inside her ball. "It's not time to awaken."

"You have all morning to sleep." I informed her and took a shirt out of the suitcase. "Snugged up tight in this shirt."

"You will not put me in there!" Her voice echoed loud and clear. "I demand it!"

"Well, so do I." I wrapped the shirt around her several times. Mr. Prince Charming lay on top of the shirt once I stuck it back in the suitcase. "You can't go." I shooed him out of the suitcase. My bracelet jingled from my wrist and I shook it toward him. "Remember, you gave me a new charm."

Rowl! He darted off in the direction of the bedroom just in time for the sound of Oscar's alarm going off.

"Rise and shine," I hollered from the family room and glanced over at the coffee pot then glanced at my hands. I shrugged. "One time," I giggled and wiggled my fingers toward the pot. Instantly, a full pot of coffee was in the carafe.

I tried to stop the big smile from creeping across my lips, but couldn't. I was feeling a little proud of the new fun gift Aunt Helena had given me and found myself wishing I had it all the time. I opened the cabinet and took out two mugs and filled them before I went back to the bedroom where Oscar was lying with a big grin on his face.

"Finally." He propped himself up on his elbows. "We are getting out of here to enjoy our honeymoon."

"Tulip Island here we come." I planted the biggest grin on my face even though my gut churned with an uneasiness.

A car horn beeped outside.

"And the Karimas are here to take us." Oscar jumped up and quickly threw on the clothes he had laid out the night before. "I knew they would be early."

"I didn't know they were taking us to the airport." I walked back down the hall with the two cups of coffee still in my hands. I set them on the small kitchen table and opened the door.

Patience and Constance Karima were standing on the threshold. Constance shook her finger, Patience followed.

"I told you to be ready." Constance tugged on the collar of her housedress. Her grey hair sat in tight curls around her round head. Her green eyes glared at me from underneath her glasses.

"Be ready," Patience repeated. She too tugged on her housedress. Everything Constance did, Patience did. The twins had soft grey curls all over their heads and small wire-rimmed glasses. They were the oldest members of Whispering Falls and they owned Two Sisters and A Funeral. They were the only funeral home in Whispering Falls and it was perfect for their gift of being ghost whisperers.

"That's right, seeester. I told them." She waddled back to the hearse that was parked next to my El Camino in front of the cottage.

"Umhmm." Patience hurried over to the hearse. "You told them."

"Where are your bags?" Constance asked.

"I'll get them." I went back inside and Oscar had the suitcases zipped and was rolling them toward the door. I looked over his shoulder and did a quick onceover around the room to make sure he hadn't seen the Magical Cures Book and potion bottle I had stuck in my bag. I didn't see either, so I was confident he didn't bother looking.

Mr. Prince Charming glared from the top of the couch.

"I know. I wish you could go." I ran my hand down his back. He didn't budge. He didn't purr. He didn't even try to bat at the dangling charm bracelet.

"He's not," Oscar said in a stern voice when he took the bags out of the cottage.

"I'll make it up to you."

"He'll be fine." Constance stood in the doorway. "And if you need us, we aren't busy for a week."

"Need you?" I asked. "You already said you'd take care of him."

"Not the cat. You." She pointed directly at me. "I hear that you are having them nightmares again and if you need us, me and my sister can come over there and help you out."

"Oh, I'm sure we'll be fine." I gulped. A sudden fear gripped around my heart like there was a hand in there squeezing the life right out of me.

Chapter Five

"Tums? Pepto? Anything?" Oscar asked. He looked a little green around the gills.

I helped him off the sea propeller plane and got him seated on the sandy beach where the plane had skidded to a stop. I dumped the contents of my bag on the beach to see if I had anything I could give him.

"Nothing," I said sympathetically. "Maybe they have something." I nodded to a grey-haired gentleman and a young red-headed woman next to him.

"Welcome, welcome to Tulip Island where all of your fantasies will come true." The man and the woman both wore white suits and black flip-flops.

He clapped his hands. A young man, also in a white suit, came out of nowhere with a tray full of filled champagne flutes.

"Whoohoo!" A brunette woman nearly knocked me over as she waved down the boy. "We need all of those!"

Drinks were the last thing Oscar and I needed. From what I had heard from him, he'd been on planes several times in his life where I'd never been on any. I opened the purse and looked down into it.

"Oh!" My eyes popped open when I found something that resembled a Tic-Tac at the bottom. I picked it up for inspection. It could've been a piece of gum. Regardless, I glanced at Oscar and his head was buried in his hands. I looked around to see if anyone else was looking at us, but they were too busy getting a lei strung around their necks and gulping up the champagne.

I rubbed the pad of my finger and thumb together while I contemplated using the finger spell technique. I mean, it would be for the good of not only a vacation, but for Oscar to feel better. Who on Earth wants to start a vacation off sick? Especially in a place like this?

I contemplated my choices while I looked around. Tulip Island was magical in a natural way. The crystal blue and green water spread for miles ahead and to the sides of me with no other land in sight. The beach was whiter than any sand I'd ever seen and the large palm leaves swayed in the light breeze making the temperature feel comfortable.

"Cheers to the bride!" One of the girls yelled with the flute lifted high in the air. A group of four women and four men gathered around and clinked their glasses.

"Cheers," I grumbled and took another last look at the mystery piece of candy or whatever was in the bottom of my bag. Without giving it much more thought. I did it. I touched the piece of whateveritwas with my finger and healing Oscar's sick tummy in my mind. The little zap transferred from my finger to the candy.

"Oh! Found a mint." I held it up between my finger and thumb, grinning ear-to-ear.

"A mint?" Oscar's eyes dipped down on the edges. "Are you kidding me? I need more than a mint."

"Oh try it." I shoved my fingers in his face. "Darla always gave me a mint to settle my stomach."

He looked up at me with a look of uncertainty on his face.

"I don't even like mint." His brows furrowed.

"You don't like an upset stomach either." I shrugged. I put my fingers to his lips. "Open up."

"June." He groaned and I took the moment to shove the mint in.

"Chew!" I demanded.

"How is everyone here?" The grey-headed man walked up. "June and Oscar Park."

"How did you know our names?" I asked in a curious, oh-my-god-did-Aunt-Helena-or-someone-tell-them-about-us way.

"I know everyone who comes to my island." The man folded his hands in front of him before he turned toward the island and opened his arms wide doing a sweep in front of him. "Ten visitors this week. The wedding party and the two of you."

"Oscar got a little sick on the plane over from the mainland." I pointed to Oscar. He was getting a little more color back in his face. "It was so gorgeous."

Flying was nothing like I expected it to be and I truly enjoyed looking down on the earth and realizing I was so much smaller than I realized.

"I'm feeling better." Oscar stood up and stretched his neck side-to-side and brought his arms above his head. "Actually feeling a lot better. Mint must be good for the bad belly."

"Mint?" The man looked at Oscar and then slid his eyes toward me.

"I had a mint in the bottom of my purse. But I'm sure we'd love a toast of your champagne." I pointed to the young man who was once again surrounded by the wedding party.

With not a second to waste, the grey-haired man lifted his arms to the side and clapped two quick times. The boy that couldn't be any more than ten years old scurried over with the tray.

"I'm Mr. Victor, your host. This is Gene, he will help you with all your needs." Mr. Victor nodded for Gene to step ahead. "That is my daughter Violet. She will help you plan all of your adventures."

We glanced over at Violet. Apparently she had tripped over her own flip-flops and the tray of champagne she'd taken over to the demanding wedding party had landed all down the bride-to-be's dress. The bride was cursing under her breath and poor Violet had turned all shades of red.

"How do we do get signed up?" I asked, hoping to keep us busy all week long. I rubbed my hand around my wrist and felt the charms.

Mr. Victor's eyes drew down to my arm. "Very nice. I hope you will be able to go to our shop and pick a nice beach charm for your bracelet."

He smiled.

"Thank you." Oscar put his arm around me and with the other took a flute off of Gene's tray and handed it to me, then got himself one. "I'm sure we are going to have a wonderful time."

"Yes." Mr. Victor's chin drew down and he gave a little head tilt before he walked back toward the tree line.

Oscar and I stood there sipping our champagne, watching all that was going on in front of us. The wedding group was rowdy, cheering and high-fiving.

"Welcome to Tulip Island." Violet walked up. This time she'd exchanged the tray of champagne for a clipboard in her hand. I couldn't help but wonder if Mr. Victor had red hair like hers and she'd gotten it from him. "I'm Violet and I will be helping you with all the island has to offer."

I looked over my shoulder to see what Violet was staring at. She was talking to us, but paying attention to the wedding party. Granted, I knew that Oscar and I were an old married couple, and I was sure the island wedding was much more fun to be a part of, but it was our honeymoon.

"Wonderful." I sucked in a deep breath and put the thoughts aside. Even though my nerves were still running through me like a live wire, I was stuck here for a few days and I guessed I had better make the best of it. "Do we sign up there?" I pointed to her clipboard.

The faster Oscar and I got into an activity, the sooner I'd feel safer.

"No, silly." Violet shoo-shooed me. "You are going to go to your villa and unwind while we do it all for you."

Inside my stomach was churning, outside my lips were smiling.

"Sounds good to me." Oscar stood up and reached over, pulling me to him. "This is the perfect way to start out our honeymoon."

"Great." Violet clapped her hands and Gene came running over. "Gene, please show the newlyweds to their villa." She used the pen to mark something off on her clipboard. "If you follow Gene, he is going to give you the guided tour to your villa and I'll see you two lovebirds back here for lunch at noon, island time." She winked before she went to give her spiel to the wedding group.

"Please follow me." Gene gestured us to follow him. I slipped off my shoes and let the sand run between my toes. It was soft and warm just how I thought it would feel.

The trail was shaded by the palm trees on each side. They were the prettiest trees I'd ever seen. In fact, Tulip Island was beautiful. At first I was upset the Order of Elders had sent us here, but now I can see they picked the perfect place.

"This is our lodge." Gene took us through the open air room. The view of the ocean was behind us and the view of a mountain was in front of us. "You will come here if you'd like the breakfast buffet as well as any sort of snacks during the day."

There was a long table with baskets made out of the rinds of watermelons and filled with all sorts of melons.

Raw shrimp skewers were stuck in an ice sculpture in the shape of a pineapple.

"Here are the offices if you should need to come see Mr. Victor or Violet for anything." We followed him down a hallway that was open to another path at the end.

Pictures of Mr. Victor and Violet, through the years, were framed on both sides of the wall. Violet's hair was even redder when she was a baby. The pictures depicted Violet's life growing up on the island. I stopped when I looked at the photos where Violet had seemed to go through a little plump stage like most girls going through puberty.

We walked out of the open building and onto the path. It took us about five minutes until we came to a fork on the trail, and Gene stopped.

"This is your path to your villa and only your path. There shouldn't be anyone walking down here but you and it's for your privacy. There are hammocks along the trail for you to stop and enjoy the breathtaking shoreline at any point."

He stopped and let his eyes wander in a simple gesture for us to follow. Gene was right. It was breathtaking. There wasn't a soul around but us and the only sound was the waves hitting the beach in a whisper, though it was so close. We followed him in silence as he continued to tell us about the non-motorized water sports on the island and we should take full advantage of the snorkeling equipment in our room because Tulip Island had the best snorkeling in the Caribbean.

"We have you down for the tiki hut dinner tonight, which is the best dining experience, in my opinion." Gene took the curve of the path to the most spectacular view.

Oscar and I stood there for about a minute and took it all in. The palm trees opened up to a small white-planked villa that stood on stilts in the middle of the ocean. There was a large wooden float anchored next to it for hours of lying around. There was a wooden bridge that extended from the sandy beach to the villa that let you cross the water, or you could swim up to the ladder of the villa.

"This is ours?" Oscar squeaked out.

"I love the reaction when I show someone this for the first time." Gene rocked on the heels of his flip-flops with a big smile on his face. "This also happens to be the quietest spot on Tulip Island. You literally never have to leave this area."

"But Violet said we had lunch at noon." I reminded them after my stomach growled.

"She also said island time." He winked just like she had.

"Island time, which means our time." Oscar grabbed my hand and dragged me toward the bridge. "Which means we can do whatever we want."

He dropped my hand and took off. I rubbed my wrist. No amount of trepidation I had was ever going to override the look on Oscar's face. He was like a kid in a candy shop.

"Here is a phone for the island." Gene handed me a small flip phone. "This will ring me or Violet for any unforeseen needs you may have, but we are pretty good at getting your needs covered before you even know what you need."

"Thank you." I couldn't take my eyes off Oscar who had taken his shoes off and was running through the tide, kicking up sand as he went along. "I think I might need a shovel and pail," I joked.

"Those are already in the villa for your pleasure." Gene didn't get the joke, but I simply thanked him again and sent him on his way.

"I can't wait to snorkel!" Oscar called from the water. He motioned for me to join him. "Come on, June! We aren't going to waste a minute."

I bit my lip and let out a heavy sigh before I took a step toward him. No matter how much of a paradise we were in, something told me that snorkeling wasn't going to be the thing I needed to do. In fact, my nightmare had told me. How was I going to tell Oscar?

Chapter Six

"There is something about not being home that makes it so good." Oscar ran his finger along my arm propping up my chin as I looked out over the water from the bed in the villa. "I love being with my wife."

"Wife." I grinned every time I heard myself being referred to as his wife. This time was even better. It came from his mouth. I stayed on my belly and looked out the open wall in front of me. The sheer curtains waved in the light breeze and the champagne and strawberries did exactly what Mr. Victor had intended them to do for us. Relax me.

"I love you, June." Oscar ran his hand down my back. "Thank you for agreeing to let go of our home life even if it is for a few days."

Next to the bed was a bottle of champagne, two flutes and a few stacked Ding Dongs that had been waiting upon our arrival.

"You're welcome." My heart filled with joy. I reached over to the table and grabbed a Ding Dong. After I unwrapped it, I took a bite and offered Oscar a bite. "What do you say we get our swimsuits on and go explore the shoreline?" I stuffed the rest of it in my mouth before I got out of bed.

Being the non-romantic person I was, I'd had enough mush for one early afternoon in what was going to be a few days of mush.

"You are hopeless," Oscar joked and got out of bed.

"I've never seen anything so fancy." I unzipped the suitcase that had been placed on the suitcase stand before we'd gotten there. I took out one angry Madame Torres. "And I've never seen anyone so mad."

Oscar looked over at me as he tied up his swim trunks.

"She's all black." I held Madame Torres up to show him. "Madame Torres, you can come out now." I tapped my fingernail on the glass ball.

"I will not." Her voice boomed from deep within. "What you have done to me should be against spiritual law."

"Really?" I asked. "I brought you to this beautiful slice of heaven on Earth and if you'd just take a peek, you'll know what I'm talking about."

Suddenly one of her purple eye shadowed eyes took up the entire glass ball. It opened, rolled around to get a view, and then narrowed when it looked at me.

"I guess I can try to come out and get over this sickness," she groaned. "Do you know what they do to your luggage at those airports?"

I shook my head.

"They open up your stuff and they look at it all. They shook me up like I was a snow globe. Snow. Globe!" she shouted. I had to turn my head so she couldn't see my smirk.

"Oh no." I put her on top of the clothes and rummaged through the rest of the suitcase. "Did they get my book?"

I hadn't thought about anyone going through my things.

"They tried to take a lot of stuff, but I had to make an appearance." An evil grin crossed her red lips, exposing her bright white teeth. "I gave them a little spook."

"Good girl." I couldn't help but laugh. "You do love me."

"I love me. I love my life and I want to go home. That means that I have to keep you safe in order to get back there. A little spook never hurt anyone." She winked. "Now, go put me over there so I can get a good view of this place while I'm here."

"Will do." I gave her a snappy salute and put her next to the bed on the table. "This will make you happy and relaxed."

I looked into the ball. Madame Torres was sitting cross-legged on a floating oriental carpet already doing mediation.

"Everything alright?" Oscar asked.

"Everything is just fine." I grabbed my bathing suit out of the suitcase and headed off to the bathroom.

While I was getting my suit on, Oscar left to go to the beach, where I found him with his toes in the surf.

"Let's take a walk and see what's down there." He pointed ahead of us and grabbed my hand.

"I'm not going to lie." I swung our hands between us as we walked down the beach to anywhere and nowhere at the same time. "This is beautiful. And I thought Whispering Falls was amazing."

"Our home is amazing, but sometimes we have to feed our own souls and just live like we used to." Oscar was right. "Don't you miss living in Locust Grove sometimes? The easy life?"

"You mean climbing in and out of my window, smashing Darla's flowers and feeding me Ding Dongs?" Those were fond memories. "No, life was hard for me. You were a cop and I was trying to make a living making homeopathic cures. I had no meaning to my life."

"You are meant to be with me." He put his arm around my shoulders as we watched the waves roll in and roll out. "As long as I have you, I know life is great."

"Me too." My wrist burned and I rubbed the charm bracelet. *And as long as I have you,* I thought as I rubbed the newest charm.

"Newlyweds, huh?" A man from the wedding party jogged up.

"We are." Oscar agreed. "Oscar and June Park."

I was going to correct him because I did technically keep my name, June Heal, but for argument's sake and the fact I didn't feel like explaining why I had kept my name, I let Oscar ramble to his new friend.

"I'm getting married tomorrow. It was her idea to bring our closest friends and it seemed like fun." The guy put his hand out. "Patrick."

They did the man shake and did some more talking as the three of us walked down the beach. I stopped every few feet and looked at the shells to see if there were any I might be able to take back with me.

"We are going snorkeling tonight if you want to go." Patrick was a friendly sort of guy. He had short blond hair. Tall. Already tan. Fairly well built.

"At night?" I asked.

"Yeah." He anxiously nodded his head. "Tulip Island has the best night fishing. There are some fish that glow in the dark. It's a lot of fun."

"You've done it before?" Oscar asked with a curious tone.

"Oh yeah, man. Me and my family used to come here all the time, so my fiancée wanted to come here." He pointed to someone off in the distance. "In fact, that's my brother. I'll see you tonight."

He didn't give us a chance to turn down his offer before he took off in a sprint toward his brother and the rest of the wedding party. They had already gathered down on the beach in their swimsuits. Drinks were flying.

"Hi!" The brunette from earlier flagged us down. "Patrick said you two were joining us for snorkeling tonight. I'm Juliette."

"Hi," I greeted her. "I'm June and this is my husband, Oscar. I hear congratulations are in order."

"We are so excited. This is the first time I've been here, but Patrick raved about it until I gave in."

"You gave in?" I asked, recalling just a few short minutes ago Patrick had told us that it was her idea to come here.

"Oh yes." She laughed. "What girl wants to give up the dream of a big church wedding to get married in a bathing suit." She shook her head. "One in love. Anyway, Patrick and his family have been coming here for years. Unfortunately, his parents were killed in a terrible house fire. Gas stove they believe exploded and that's why Patrick won't get a gas oven." Her brows furrowed. "Terrible really. And now it's just the two of them. Peter and Patrick."

"It's just me and Oscar. Both of our parents are deceased and we have no siblings." The wedding party looked like they were having all sorts of fun without the bride. "Who is that out there?" I wanted to change the subject when I saw a pair of flippers pierce the water in the distance.

"Oh, that's Peter. My soon-to-be brother-in-law." She shifted her weight and folded her arms. "He was really affected by the death of his parents. They coddled him a lot and he was in the home when his parents died. In fact, Patrick was the one who found him almost dead in the basement and saved his life."

"Really?" I couldn't imagine what that must've been like.

"Yes. So now we have custody of him, though he's going to be eighteen in a few months." She let out a heavy sigh. "He didn't want to come because he hates to be in crowds. Patrick reminded him that Tulip Island was secluded. When he saw you and Oscar getting on the plane, he freaked."

"That's so sad." I really wanted Peter to be happy and for a split second I wondered if I could do a little spell to help him.

"He's special." She smiled and waved at him when he saw us looking at him. He waved back with something in his hand.

"Special?" I asked.

"He needed help all through school and went to special schools." Juliette smiled.

"Oh." I lifted my chin in the air. I wasn't sure what to say.

"Anyway, I insist that you come to the rehearsal dinner before snorkeling and you must come to the wedding." She tapped my arm. A pulse of lightning rushed through me, causing me to catch my breath.

"Sure," Oscar confirmed. "It's just us on this island so we might as well make the most fun of it."

He looked at me. I felt sorry for him because I could relate to how he had to be feeling, thinking about losing his parents at a young age like me.

"Of course we will." My mouth dried. "We wouldn't miss the dinner, snorkeling or the wedding."

"Wonderful." She bounced on the balls of her feet. "I'll be sure to tell Mr. Victor to include you in all the details. I'd better get back to the group. Would you like to join us?"

"I think we are going to continue to walk around and take a look at the beautiful island." Oscar took me by the hand. "We will see you tonight."

"You two are so cute." Her button nose curled and she scurried off, back to their group of eight.

"What was that about?" Oscar asked. "You looked frightened."

"Not frightened." I made myself smile at him. Playfully I kicked up the water on him. "I thought it was our honeymoon and it was supposed to be just us." I snuggled him closer by putting my arm in the crook of his. "Not us and another couple. And we were supposed to have dinner at the tiki place Gene talked about."

"We have the next few days alone. We can be cordial and reschedule dinner." Oscar's manners was one thing I had fallen in love with years ago. "Maybe we can be like Patrick and make this a family thing."

"Hey!" I punched him in the arm. "You know I don't want children."

It'd come to be a bad topic over the past couple of months since we got married. After all we'd been through, finding out we were spiritualists, we had decided that children weren't an option in our future. I was sticking to that. But leave it to Oscar to be all emotional about family and family traditions.

"Never say never." Oscar smacked me on the tushie and ran out to sea, diving into the depths of the sea green ocean.

"Never!" I yelled as his head bobbed up out of the water and I popped a squat in the sand. "I said it! Never!"

I barely got my toes buried and my book out of my bag when I heard yelling behind me. It was hard to make out what they were saying with sound of the waves crashing up against the beach. But there was some crying.

I looked back and saw Patrick. His head was bobbing back and forth, first finger pointing, then rubbing his hands together and finally nervously running his hands through his hair.

"I love you. This is right. You and I both know it." He assured her, (I'm assuming her was Juliette).

I'd heard of cold feet before, but I never experienced it. My only issue when I got married was not having my parents with me.

Evidently, Patrick made it all better with more words because when I turned back around, they were in each other's arms, playing kissy face. I couldn't see Juliette's face, but I could see the smile on Patrick's face. It was the first time that my intuition told me that he was really in love. I turned back around to watch Oscar's feet bob up and out of the water from all his diving.

"Boys will be boys." Juliette appeared next to me.

"Hi," I said. The line between my eyes creased. There was no way she'd had time to walk from the palm tree to here within seconds.

"You look confused." She laughed. "Juliette. I just met you back there." She pointed behind her.

"Yes. I know. Weren't you just. . ." I blinked my eyes a couple of times. I noticed the bag in her hand. "Where have you been?"

"Looking for treasure." She giggled.

"Treasure?" I asked, a little curious.

"That's what I'm told by Peter." She held up a map that had been drawn by what looked to be a child. "He claims his dad told him about it. He insisted we go up to the volcano and look for it. Since Patrick was going to play around here, I thought I'd go and play with Peter."

"That is so sweet." I noticed Peter was looking through his own bag of treasure. He pulled out a bottle of chocolate milk and sat in the sand to drink it. "Well?"

"Well what?" she asked.

"Did you find any treasure?" I asked.

"He found some beautiful treasure, didn't you, Peter?" Juliette's smile was tender and caring. "Put down your milk and show Mrs. Park what you found. He loves chocolate milk."

"June," I corrected her. "You can call me June." I gulped realizing more than ever that I had taken on the same attitude as Darla and how she didn't like to be called anything but Darla.

I sat up on the edge of the beach chair and watched the pride on Peter's face as he gently took out of the bag different colored shells.

"Treasure." He held out a beautiful piece of lava rock that had solidified.

"That's beautiful." I pushed myself up a little more to get a better look.

"He had the most beautiful shell collection from all the times his parents had brought him here, but lost it all in the fire." She rubbed a loving hand down Peter's back. He didn't seem to pay much attention to it.

My heart warmed. It was good to see Juliette taking on the mothering role for her soon-to-be brother-in-law.

"I hope you find a lot of treasure," I said to him and looked over when I heard the sand shuffling behind me.

"Treasure?" Violet asked as she stood behind us.

"Yeah." Juliette laughed. "Peter thinks there is treasure near the volcano."

"The volcano is off limits." Violet didn't find the cute treasure hunt at all cute. "Gene should've told you that when he took you to your villa."

"He did, but we were fine." Juliette drew back.

"If it weren't off limits, then we would take you. Stay away from the volcano." Violet's voice was stern, not at all wavering.

"Chill out." Juliette shook her head.

"Everything okay here?" Patrick jogged up. He looked at Juliette with the dead eyes I'd seen before.

"It's fine." Juliette kissed his lips. His eyes wandered to Violet and the look of love glistened in them as he looked at her.

"It's not fine." Violet turned on the balls of her bare feet and trotted off.

Patrick and Juliette strolled off. Juliette kicking the surf water up at Patrick as he grabbed her, picked her up and cradled her in his arms.

"This is when I tell my father that sometimes it's best to just shut down the island." Anger spilled out of Violet's mouth. She had returned and sat next to me. In the sunlight, the freckles danced across her nose and even along the tops of her shoulders.

"It's a beautiful treasure not to share with the world." I dragged my bag across the sand and took out my sunscreen.

"People like her will make it not so beautiful." Violet's eyes narrowed. "Plus, Patrick should've told her because he and his family have been here so many times that they know what is off limits."

Her displeasure of Juliette was apparent and I wasn't so sure it was the fact that Juliette had gone past the preserve and to the volcano that was the true source of her hatred or the fact Juliette had snagged Patrick.

"That smells good." She turned her attention to me and adjusted the elastic of the strapless dress underneath her armpits. "What is it?"

I held out the lime green potion bottle.

"It's sunscreen. Homeopathic sunscreen." I had to tell her something due to the fact it wasn't bottled in the normal sunscreen plastic containers.

"Homeopathic?" Her head tilted. She took it from me and got a closer inspection. She even popped the cork to get a smell. "What is the SPF?"

The question swirled in my head. The potion was specifically made for me and it took on the SPF that my body and skin needed.

"I'm not sure. I have been testing it out for years and it's something I make for me so it's not the same for you." I shrugged hoping the answer would satisfy her.

"Interesting." She turned the bottle around and got a look at it from all sides. "Can I try some?"

"Sure." I backed up in the chair and started to relax. The ocean was calm and bright blue with a hint of green every so often. In the distance a family of dolphins took turns jumping in and out of the water.

The water flowed beyond the horizon while the baby blue sky blanketed above us with a few puffs of white clouds that looked as if someone had pulled apart a cotton ball and placed them there. The chirp of the seagulls echoed as they flew overhead and the sound of the waves lightly rolling on the packed sand was so soothing to the soul.

As much as I hated to admit it, the Order of Elders did send us to a wonderful island for our honeymoon and I was not disappointed.

"This is wonderful." Violet had taken it upon herself to pour some of the sunscreen in her hands and apply it to her bare shoulders. "Silky smooth." Her hands slid along her arms. "Are you a scientist?"

"Not really." I had never really thought about it, but I would say the mortals might call me that. I dug back in my bag and took out my round brush. It made the most perfect curl at the end of my bob. "You know healing medicines?" She nodded. "Well, I'm a homeopathic scientist, I guess you could say. I make my own cures for things."

"Do you sell them?" She handed the bottle back to me. Curiosity sat in her eyes.

"I do. Back home in Kentucky I have a shop called A Charming Cure." My stomach tickled with excitement. I hadn't really left Whispering Falls enough to brag on my business since opening it. "It's mostly word of mouth and I also have a little line in Head to Toe Works."

"Oh. I love those stores." Her eyes lit up. "You must be famous."

"No, not really." Only in the spiritual world, I thought, knowing that I used to be the Village President and the chosen one at one point. "But I do love my job."

"Oscar is too?" she asked.

"Oh no." My nose curled. He's a wizard; I smiled as the thought breezed along my brain. "He's a cop. For the same village."

"You live in a village?" She continued to hammer me with questions, making me think that I should've used more common names.

"Small town in Kentucky. It's really a tourist town set in the foothills of the caves and mountains." I leaned my head back on the lawn chair and closed my eyes, hoping she'd take a hint and leave.

"That is wonderful." She paused. "My father never has taken me to the states."

"Really?" I was a little shocked. "You know how to run a nice business for never leaving."

"When I was younger, his excuse was that the world would swallow me whole. It scared me, but really he needed the help." She smiled. "I got my education right here. I learned to sew." She ran her hands down her sundress.

"You made that?" I asked.

"I did and I love it. In fact, all the suits and clothes we wear on the island are made by me." She nodded. Pride was written all over her face.

"I love your dress." I noticed the detail in the stitching and the perfect hemline. The side seams were evenly matched with the chevron pattern. "Did you do the monogramming too?"

She ran her hand across the monogram on the small pocket on the chest.

"I did." She smiled. She pointed to my brush. "That just made the perfect curl."

Without asking, she ran it through her hair a couple of times, leaving the end turned under.

"How on earth?" she smiled.

"As seen on TV." I lied. Chandra had given me the brush and it was special. No matter where I was, I could run the brush through my hair and it would look perfect after every stroke.

Her flip phone buzzed and she walked away to answer it. In the distance I could see Patrick and Juliette walking down the beach. He looked over his shoulder and back at me. I guessed I wasn't interesting enough, because his eyes drew behind me.

I looked over my shoulder to see what he was looking at. Violet disappeared behind the palm tree where I'd seen Patrick talking to someone. When she peaked around, the pair of eyes the person Patrick had been talking to was Violet not Juliette. My mouth dropped and my stomach knotted.

I dragged my bag across the sand back to me and stuck my hand in. I pulled out the foil covered Ding Dong and opened it. As soon as my teeth cracked the hard outside shell of the delicious treat, I couldn't help but think of what I'd heard Patrick say and it wasn't to Juliette.

I love you.

Chapter Seven

"I'm telling you something is going on." I just couldn't keep my mouth shut as much as I wanted to. I had to tell Oscar exactly what I'd seen. "He is with another woman. And it's Violet."

"That's ridiculous, June." Oscar was in the shower while I stood at the mirror putting on makeup for the rehearsal dinner for Patrick and Juliette. "He was all gushy about them getting married while we were in the water."

"I'm telling you I saw it with my own eyes. He was kissing Violet. He told her he loved her. And Juliette can't marry him like that." Even though I didn't really know them and I really shouldn't be sticking my nose into their business, I was still a woman that wasn't about to sit around and watch another woman destroy a marriage that hadn't even begun yet. "I'd rather her know now instead of years down the road."

The eyes.

"June," Oscar stepped out of the shower and toweled himself off. "This is none of our business. In a few days we will never see these people again."

"But. . ." I protested.

"But nothing." He walked over and kissed the top of my head. "Did you see Violet and Patrick actually kissing? Her full face?"

"No." I wanted to tell him that my intuition told me and that her eyes told me and his face told me, but then he'd say I was using my gift and that I was supposed to have left it at home.

"We are on our honeymoon. They have nothing to do with us. If you can't handle that then we will do our own thing tonight." He pulled back and looked at me.

"No. I told Juliette we would go." Not that I was desperate to keep my word, I was desperate to find out what was going on with Violet and Patrick. I dug through my bag looking for my brush. "Why would he marry Juliette if he is in love with another woman?"

"June." Oscar put on a blue button down and buttoned it from the bottom up. I gave up on finding the brush and walked over and turned his collar down. "Honey, please let it go. This is none of our business and you aren't home to make a potion to find out."

"Potion," I whispered.

"No. No magic." His brows lifted. "You promised."

I rubbed the pad of my finger and thumb together. "No potions."

But I never said I wouldn't touch Patrick with my new finger spell gift from Aunt Helena and give him a little jolt of a love spell to be in love and stay in love with Juliette.

I never said no magic. I smiled and curled up on my toes to give him a kiss. He hesitated and looked deep within my soul through my eyes, then gave in.

"And this night snorkeling is going to be a lot of fun." His eyes danced with excitement.

"Yeah." There was trepidation in my voice. "I think I'll let you go and I'll hang here to enjoy the nighttime view."

He smiled and kissed the top of my head. He knew I wasn't going to go. I had never been fond of doing things outside of my surroundings, especially in the middle of the night in a big dark ocean. The *Jaws* theme song played in my head.

"Da-duh, da-duh." I teased Oscar doing my best *Jaws* impression as he flailed his body like he was being attacked. We laughed as I grabbed my bag and he waited by the door.

Tulip Island was just as magical at night as it was in the daylight. The stars blanketed the sky like all the fireflies that dotted the night in Whispering Falls. The ocean and breeze played around in a flirtatious motion, in sync with one another.

My soul had settled down a little since the first day was almost over and there wasn't anything that sent my gut on high alert. I'd taken a sneak peek at A Charming Cure through Madame Torres. She was happy sitting on the table looking out at the ocean during the day, so she was very accommodating to my request without a snarky attitude. She even showed me a very grumpy Mr. Prince Charming sitting next to The Gathering Rock while Patience Karima tried to lure him with the fresh head of a salmon. Little did she realize, Mr. Prince Charming hated all things fishy. Or any cat food for that matter.

"Do you regret the impromptu wedding ceremony we had?" Oscar asked once the view of the rehearsal dinner was in our sights. He paused and continued as though he were trying to change the original question. "I mean, like the wedding you always dreamed of?"

"This isn't what Juliette said she always dreamed of." I pointed to the white tent that was set up on the beach. White twinkling lights covered the top and the poles, so much so that you couldn't even see the material the tent was made out of.

Mr. Victor and Violet were standing on the outside of the tent talking with a couple of the people in the wedding party. He made eye contact with me and acknowledged it with a little nod.

"Patrick said it was her dream." Oscar refused to believe what she'd told me.

"I told you that she said it was his because he'd come here so much with his family and it was to honor them. But I don't care about them." I hooked my arm in the crook of his elbow and pulled him to me. "I had the most beautiful wedding."

"That wasn't my question." Oscar stopped. The full moon was like a spotlight on us. "God, you are beautiful." He ran the back of his hand down my cheek. "I love you so much."

"I love you too." I snuggled my head up against his chest and held him for a few minutes.

"Are you enjoying your honeymoon?" Violet walked up behind us.

"We are," Oscar answered her while I continued to enjoy the moment of his sentimental side. It was nice not to have the guarded cop personality like he'd have at home.

"Wonderful." She swayed side-to-side. I pulled away from Oscar. "June, you really should come to get a spa treatment."

"You can come with us!" Juliette had snuck up on us. "I'm having a treatment for the girls tomorrow."

"Come, come, everyone." Mr. Victor waved us over. "It's time for the wine tasting and for Patrick to pick the wine for the bride."

Everyone gathered around and watched as Mr. Victor did his unusual wine opening ritual where he poured, swirled, smelled, swirled again, and then took a sip before swirling another time. After he sipped and swirled, he spit into the spittoon. Violet wasn't as dramatic as her father, but she did the same thing before they let Patrick spit and swirl until he came to the conclusion that the fifth wine they tried was the perfect one.

"I have some pretty shells." Peter appeared out of nowhere and he pulled a few shells from the pocket of his pants along with some sand. "My mom and dad always loved to go shelling here. Well, not here." He pointed out to the ocean. "There. Sparkly shells."

"I see you made a new friend." Patrick walked up to us. He handed me a glass of wine. "I hope you enjoy the sweet floral notes. Juliette loves a sweet wine so I knew she'd enjoy this one."

A sneeze escaped me.

"Here." Patrick pulled out a handkerchief. "Bless you."

"Thank you." I waved the monogrammed hanky away. "I don't need. . .*achoo!*"

"I insist." He forced me to take the hanky and I couldn't help but notice it was the same stitching Violet had used on her dress.

"I couldn't use your monogrammed hanky." I held my finger under my nose, feeling yet another sneeze.

"I insist." He refused to take it back.

"Please take it." Juliette rushed over. "He has so many at home. I keep asking him where on Earth did he get them, but he keeps saying that he doesn't remember."

"I'm sure my mom had them made." His voice was reserved. His eyes shifted. "Go on Peter. It's probably your bedtime."

Peter glared at Patrick and shuffled his feet in the sand.

I noticed how he'd dismissed Peter. Peter hung his head and walked away. While Patrick made small talk, I watched Peter walk over to one of the tables and sit down. He lined his shells up on the table in front of him by size. Biggest to smallest.

"Thank you for the hanky." I tried to be as polite as I could but didn't like how I felt when he had dismissed Peter. But I didn't live in their shoes, so I decided to go with it. I tucked the hanky in my bag and put aside the idea that Violet had by chance made Patrick these hankies. I didn't know anything about monogramming or the thread that was used and I was sure that it was probably a coincidence. At least that's what I told my intuition so it would calm down and I could keep my promise to Oscar. No intuition, which was part of the whole package of me that he wanted to leave behind.

I was not good at pretending to be a mortal now that I was no longer one.

"I hope you are still going snorkeling with us tonight." Patrick looked out to the calm sea.

"I'm not so sure about the darkness." My insides shuddered for the first time in hours. It had to be the memory of the nightmare that still haunted me. I ran my hand over my bracelet and felt calm. "Oscar is definitely going to go."

Oscar did exactly what he was good at. He meandered around the tent and talked to everyone. I enjoyed watching him laughing and enjoying the time off from the reality of where we came from. He was going to do the night snorkeling with the others.

I was tired and bed was calling my name. I dismissed myself from the group and took the beach all the way around for the scenic route. I walked the water's edge and let my toes feel the warmth of the Caribbean Sea tickle them.

"It is a lovely evening." Mr. Victor stood on the beach. "Hello, June. I hope you are having a wonderful visit to our little slice of paradise."

"I am, thank you." I walked up the beach to greet him. "Oscar is really having a great time and that makes me happy."

"We hope that you are having a renewal of spirit. It's time for you take care of you and your soul." He pointed to my core.

"Thank you, Mr. Victor. I enjoy seeing Oscar happy. That fills my soul." There was something about Mr. Victor and how he wanted me to pour my soul to him that made me uncomfortable. I'm sure he wanted people to feel the magic of the island and get the most out of it. "I think I'll do the spa tomorrow before the wedding."

"Good call." He rocked back on his heels. "Ah, you know my good friend, Peter." He did a quick intro when Peter walked up.

"Hi again, Peter." I gave a slight wave. "How was treasure hunting?" I asked to make some conversation.

"Good night, Ms. Heal." Mr. Victor dismissed me, telling me it was time for me to go. He took Peter by the elbow and pulled him a little closer to him.

"Good night." I nodded and got on my way, but not without thinking that Mr. Victor's behavior was a tad bit strange.

A little way down the beach, I turned and looked over my shoulder. The party was still going strong under the tent and Mr. Victor was still standing where I'd left him, staring at me. When the moonlight hit his eyes just right, a spark flew from his eyes before his eyes became the shape of a diamond.

I hurried back to the villa and slipped into my nightgown before I got into the bed. I laid on my belly and put Madame Torres on the bed in front of me. I ran my palm over her ball.

"And just how are you enjoying yourself?" she asked in a silky voice.

"It's fine. I'm still a bit on edge about my nightmare, but so far so good." I smiled at her. "I'm glad you are here because I need some girlfriend time."

"You mean Oscar isn't all he's cracked up to be?" she asked with a hint of sarcasm.

"He's everything and more." I rested my chin on the back of my clasped hands. "But girlfriends are good too. Besides, can't you take a compliment that I like you?"

"I like you too." Her voice was crisp and clear. Small hearts floated around her ball.

"Cute." I giggled and tapped the ball with my finger thinking of Mr. Prince Charming.

"Him again?" She groaned and let her ball go to Whispering Falls where Mr. Prince Charming was still sitting next to The Gathering Rock.

"What is he doing?" I was starting to get concerned since he hadn't moved since we last looked there.

"Who knows? Crazy cat." Madame Torres voice was uncompromising yet gentle. "I'm sure he misses you as much as you miss him. Neither of you have been without the other since he showed up on your doorstep."

She was right. She and I didn't have the special bond that me and my fairy-god cat had. He probably felt like I had abandoned him.

"Here handsome." Petunia came into view of the glass ball. Mr. Prince Charming walked up to her after she sat cross-legged next to the rock. She was feeding him snacks. He looked happy. He loved her and he especially loved it when she brushed him.

I watched as Petunia rubbed and loved on him, falling asleep in the process.

The shells. The voice that dug deep in my soul floated around me as the swirling orange water curled around me. My skin crawled as if there were spiders all over me as the swirl started at my legs and wrapped around my core until it stopped tight at my neck.

"Help me," the voice called, followed by a sharp bright light. My eyes slid over and across the light until it ended, in the eyes of . . .Patrick.

"No!" I sat straight up in the bed. The wind whipped around the curtains of the open villa. In the distance lightning cracked the sky before it opened up and water poured down.

Sweat poured off of my head. My breathing was shallow. My heart thumped deep inside of me. I put a hand on Oscar's side of the bed, happy he was there.

"Patrick," I whispered. I had to get to him. I had to put a protection spell on him.

The suitcase was unzipped making it easy for me to open it and grab the small potion bottle and Magical Cures Book I'd brought with me. Without thinking, or changing out of my long white, flowing nightgown, I ran out into the pouring rain.

The lightning cracking over my head didn't help matters. I ran as fast as I could with the ingredients tucked under my arm. My bare feet smacked the battened down wet sand. The angry sea crashed along the shore with a fierce push toward the land.

"I will not!" The woman's voice screamed above the thunder. "He loves me!" Her voice was rough with anxiety.

Abruptly I stopped and turned away from the roaring sea to see Mr. Victor staring at me as a figure in a billowy dress ran away from him toward the resort. His eyes were icy and unresponsive.

A blood-curdling scream broke the tension between us just as the rain suddenly stopped. I looked down the beach where the moonlight had Juliette in its grasp. She was standing over Patrick's body that looked as though it had washed up on the beach.

Chapter Eight

"No, no." Juliette shook in disbelief as the coroner from the mainland placed Patrick on the gurney to carry him to the Coast Guard's chopper to take his body to the morgue.

There was a blanket draped around her and her friends gripped the edges so it wouldn't fall off of her. Peter sat on the beach, hugging his knees as he rocked himself back and forth. The remaining two men were in a huddle shaking their heads and trying to come up with what had happened.

"We went snorkeling and it was fine." One of the men from the wedding party told the police officer. "Violet brought us back on the boat after we snorkeled. We all said goodnight and the next thing I know; I'm woken up by Juliette's scream."

The groomsmen told the same story as Oscar. They were all staying together in one of the larger villas and Gene was able to confirm their alibis since he'd brought them more drinks.

"Patrick was going to join us for a drink because it was his last night of freedom before the wedding, but when he didn't show up, we figured he and Juliette had made other plans," his voice trailed off as he watched the helicopter lift off the beach and propel itself up in the air.

"Are you okay?" Oscar asked.

"No. I'm not." The chilly tone swept across my lips. "I knew that this was going to happen. I knew it before we got here. I knew it when we got here."

"June, this is not magic. This is not for us to be concerned with." Oscar had put his cop hat right back on his head as though we were in Whispering Falls.

"What happened?" I asked. No matter how much I tried to ignore my intuition, I couldn't ignore the tug in my stomach for a Ding Dong.

"We went snorkeling. We had a good time. When we pulled back to shore, he said that he was going to go see Juliette before he joined us for drinks." Oscar chewed the side of his cheek. I could tell he was pondering what might've really happened.

"Then take me home. I want to leave now." There was no denying my feelings. I didn't want to be here. "I can see the look on your face. You are telling me to stay out of it, but your gut is talking to you and you won't be able to stay out of it either."

"Good evening." The officer came over and interrupted us. "I understand that you are a law enforcement officer in Kentucky."

"Officer Oscar Park." Oscar and the cop shook hands. "Do you have an initial cause of death?"

"It was a drowning. According to everyone here, he was a good swimmer, but you know, the tide can turn on a good swimmer at any moment." We all looked out to the sea that was as calm as could be.

It was as though the storm came to claim Patrick's life and once it had it, the storm left.

"But I never rule anything out." He gestured to the wedding group. "The fiancée said that she had fallen asleep and when she woke up she thought he should've been back from his bachelor get together but he wasn't. So she came down to the beach to see if he'd fallen asleep down here and that's when she found him."

"Let me know if there is anything I can do." Oscar's jaw tensed. I could see all the relaxation the island had given him was no longer visible.

"I was hoping you'd say that." The officer looked at Oscar. "I'd like you to poke around, see what you can come up with. I have a hunch this was no accident."

"Why is that?" Oscar asked.

"According to Mr. Victor, Patrick knew this island almost as well as he did since he'd been coming here for years." He looked over at me. His eyes gleaned like a glassy volcanic rock. "If that's the case, Patrick knew how to swim with the undercurrent. He knew the pattern of the sea and the island."

Oscar put his hands on his hips and stood with his legs apart. His eyes skimmed the sea before he peered down at me.

"I'd be happy to take a look around." He held out his hand and they shook again.

"I'll be in touch." The officer walked away and over to the wedding group.

"Did you think I wouldn't see the Magical Cures Book?" Oscar asked in a harsh, raw voice.

"I had another nightmare and it was Patrick's face that came into view. I knew I had to do something but it was too late." I gulped back the tears. My emotions were running high from the death of Patrick and the disappointment I could see on Oscar's face.

"I asked you no magic. You agreed. You promised me." The bitterness spilled over into his voice. "Me and you. Oscar and June. No magic."

He walked off in the opposite direction of the investigation. I ran alongside him.

"Sometimes I hate our spiritual life," his voice grated harshly. "I loved June Heal. The June Heal that blew up her mom's shed a few times until it totally exploded. The June Heal that chowed down on Ding Dongs under the oak tree in my front yard."

"That June grew up," I stated matter-of-factly. "I, we, followed our fate. We didn't have a choice."

He walked faster and faster.

"You were into moving to Whispering Falls as much as me. If I recall," my voice hardened ruthlessly, "you were the one who told me to give it a try and that you were moving to take the job there. It was you who changed our fate. Not me!"

I stopped and let him stalk off into the villa. I was sure my words hurt him, but his words hurt me. It wasn't like I could turn my gift off and on like it was not part of me.

"Oh my God." I gulped. "It is who I am."

For the first time, it was as though I had fully accepted who I was.

The realization washed over me like the waves washing over the sandy beach. My old life was like the sand. The more the magic washed over me on a daily basis, the old me was washed away. The old June from Locust Grove was gone.

A spark flew from the tip of my finger. My eyes sharpened as they pierced the sea. As soon as a vision of an old trunk popped into my head, a bolt of lightning shot from the sky, knocking my world into darkness.

Chapter Nine

"Maid!" The woman's voice woke me up. "Maid service!"

I ignored the woman, glanced over at Oscar's side of the bed and found a note. He'd already gotten up to go do some investigative work. He was going to have breakfast with Officer Teabody. He also wrote that he loved me and would catch up with me.

The small flip phone Mr. Victor had given me rang.

"Hello," I asked in a low composed tone even though my insides were frozen.

"This is the maid. Can you please open up so we can clean?" The voice was more demanding than asking. The maid hung up the phone before I could protest. The sun was shining and the sea was calm as if nothing had happened last night. A deep secret was held underneath the surface. Madame Torres's globe swirled along with the waves as though she were on vacation.

Only I knew we weren't. There were clues in my dreams and if Oscar was helping out, maybe I could uncover those clues.

The maid knocked on the door louder and louder.

"I'm coming." I groaned and stalked over to the door. I flung it open and asked, "What kind of resort is this if I have to get up?"

Mr. Prince Charming darted into the room, immediately doing figure eights around my ankles. I grabbed him and snugged him to me.

"Patience?" Shock and awe blanketed me. Then a sigh of relief escaped me. Not that if I had a choice I'd chose Patience, but seeing just about anyone from home made me happy.

"Happy to see you too." Her voice was flat and condescending. "I didn't have a choice. The Order of Elders made me and sister come since we didn't have any live ones at the funeral home." She giggled and said, "Or should I say dead ones?"

"Get in here." I tucked Mr. Prince Charming under one arm and pulled her in with another one.

"The Order doesn't understand why death follows you wherever you go. And they expect me to clean you up?" Patience tsked and waddled past me. "Now I have to pretend to be a maid in order for me to help you help Oscar so you can go home on time."

"What do you mean?" I thought no matter what, we'd be leaving in a few days like we had planned.

"Wizard By-Laws state that if there is a crime committed and a spiritualist is present, the crime has to be solved before the spiritualist can go back to the life before, meaning. . ." She eased down into the chair; her housedress crept up along her shins, exposing her knee-highs rolled down to her ankles.

"Meaning we have to stay here until we figure out who murdered Patrick," my voice trailed off. "Murdered."

"Yes, he was murdered." Patience confirmed what I already knew but didn't want to say until the coroner had confirmed my suspicions or even my nightmare. "And I'm not a beach person, so we need to get to it."

"Oh dear, that was a short-lived vacation," Madame Torres's words were cool and clear as ice water.

Rowl, Mr. Prince Charming jumped out of my arms and jumped on the bed. He used both paws to bat at my crystal ball.

"I don't have time for you two to fight," I scolded them. "We've got to figure out what's happened to Patrick and who killed him."

I rushed into the bathroom and turned on the shower.

"Any clues so far?" Patience asked above the sound of the shower.

"Well, there isn't much to know. Patrick's parents died in a horrendous house fire. Patrick found his brother Peter in the basement and saved his life. Patrick (and Juliette once they were married) had guardianship of Peter even though Peter is about to have his eighteenth birthday. Other than that." I scrubbed the shampoo in my hair before I let it flow out of my bobbed locks and pondered on whether or not I should mention to her that I'd caught Patrick kissing Violet and that he happened to have the monogrammed handkerchiefs. Was it all a coincidence? My intuition told me that I needed to explore the possibility that Violet killed him.

"Sister is working on trying to get some footage of the beach from Mr. Victor, but he doesn't seem to be forthcoming," her voice carried.

"How on Earth did he accept you on the island?" To my knowledge, Mr. Victor, Violet, and Gene were the only employees on the island and they did it all. "And Mr. Prince Charming? I clearly remember Izzy telling me about animals and quarantine."

"The Order of Elders told sister and me not to worry about that," she called back.

"Patience." I turned the water off and grabbed a towel. "I'm glad you are here."

"Happy to help, only you need to hurry up. There might be a dead body waiting for me and sister at home and you are holding us up." She waddled over to the door. "I'm going to go see if sister found anything out. You know what to do. If you need us, just use that flip phone."

I grinned and nodded. I loved seeing Patience doing her own thing, rather than taking orders from her twin. There were glimpses of her being her own person while we were in Whispering Falls, but not as determined as she was now.

"Remember, I hate the sand, so the quicker the better." She walked off, her housedress hitched up on the right side of her body, her glasses cockeyed on her nose. I tried not to giggle.

"I'm so glad you are here." I turned back to look at Mr. Prince Charming who was now sitting on the table next to Madame Torres. He was either mesmerized by the beautiful scene or ignoring me. "I guess we need to go get some breakfast."

It was merely a suggestion. I wanted to go and see what was happening with the investigation and Juliette. I could only imagine her devastation. Without haste, I grabbed the Magical Cures Book and the bottle of potion and put it in my bag before strapping it across my body and headed out.

The sand was hot under my bare feet. It didn't seem to bother Mr. Prince Charming as he darted in and out of the wet sand to the dry sand. Evidence of last night's storm was nowhere to be seen. The day was as bright as it had been yesterday and the sea was again calm. In the distance, the dolphins were playing as though they were synchronized swimmers.

The rehearsal tent had been replaced by police tape that was wrapped around wooden stakes and stuck into the sand. I turned to go up the path toward the lodge where Violet had told me breakfast was served and noticed Juliette comforting Peter as they sat on a hammock with their legs dangling over. They seemed to be consoling one another so I slipped up the path to the open seating area where Officer Teabody and Oscar were huddled over a couple cups of coffee.

Mr. Prince Charming jumped up on the table and Teabody nearly leapt out of his skin. He shooed the cat away, but Mr. Prince Charming looked at him as if he had two heads.

"What's wrong with that cat? Go!" Teabody flung his wrist and tried to shoo him away again. "Go."

"I'm sorry." I hurried over and grabbed my fairy-god cat and avoided Oscar's scowl. I put him on the ground. "He has no boundaries. Ornery cat."

Mewl, Mr. Prince Charming sat next to Oscar and began to lick the sand off of his paws before he rubbed them over each ear.

"Excuse us." Oscar stood up, nearly kicking the cat, and grabbed me by the arm before he dragged me over to the breakfast buffet.

"This looks delicious." I jerked my arm out of his grip. "I think I'll have French toast."

"I should've known you snuck that cat in." Oscar's accusing words stung me. "Not able to keep your promise to me. When are you going to take our marriage seriously?"

"You think I did this?" I asked in a whisper. "Think again."

"The quicker I help them, the quicker we can enjoy the honeymoon." Oscar wasn't telling me anything I didn't already know.

"Do they have any leads?" I asked.

"The only thing the initial autopsy found was some hair in his grip and under his nails." Oscar bit the side of his lip. "It wasn't his hair or Juliette's. It was red."

"Red?" My eyes bounced wide open. "As in Violet's red?"

Oscar nodded.

Oscar looked into the distance as if he were logging in his head what I was saying.

"Did you question Violet?" I asked because that seemed like the obvious thing to do. "Because I was thinking she might've had something to do with it."

"Thinking or?" He pointed to my gut.

"Yea." Sheepishly I looked down and shuffled my feet. "I can't help it, Oscar."

"I know." He let out a deep sigh. "As much as I wanted to leave our magic at home, it just seems to follow. I'm sorry for snapping at you." I was glad to see he was starting to see it my way. "What are you thinking?"

"I told you I saw them kissing. Then he told her he loved her." I clearly heard that and I wasn't going to believe it only was my active imagination. "Violet had much displeasure, almost hatred toward Juliette when she found out Juliette had taken Peter to the volcano to look for Peter's treasure on the map he'd drawn as a child."

"Juliette is just being the mother."

"I know that and you know that, but Violet was so mad and said that Patrick knew better since he'd been coming here all his life and that area was off limits." My eyes shifted to make sure no one else was around. "I think there was something going on between Violet and Patrick or that some little vacation fling happened between them. Violet even made him those monogrammed handkerchiefs."

"So they had a teenage fling or something." Oscar shrugged. "So what?"

"To Violet that is everything. He is everything. She also told me that she's never left this island. She only knows the feelings she has or had for Patrick. When she saw Patrick and Juliette together, getting married right here under her nose." I smacked my hands together. "Boom. She lost her mind and killed him."

"She does know the island better than anyone and knows the ocean and the patterns of the sea." Oscar couldn't deny the fact that my conclusion made sense. "Officer Teabody said that he had a meeting scheduled with Mr. Victor and Violet about it after the breakfast buffet is closed." He glanced over my shoulder and looked out into the trees where you could barely see Pete and Juliette in the hammock.

"Did you talk to Juliette?" he asked.

I shook my head, "No, she looked like she was consoling Peter. But I do plan to offer my condolences." My lips thinned.

"Well, just this once." Oscar's eyes warned me as well as the tone in his voice. "If she does give you any information that sets off an alarm to why anyone would want to kill Patrick, you can ask her questions."

"Deal." My lips turned into a big grin. His idea of information and how to gather it was far different from my idea of gathering information.

Mewl, Mr. Prince Charming darted up on his hind legs and batted at my dangling charms.

"Where did he come from?" Oscar demanded in a low tone.

"Would you like some syrup?" the familiar voice asked from behind the buffet table.

"Constance." Oscar jaw dropped when he saw it was Constance Karima holding the syrup ladle.

"How are you?" she asked in a pleasant, yet stern voice. "The Order of Elders sent us to make sure June wasn't accused of yet another murder." She leaned in and waved the ladle between her and Oscar, "You and I both know that June has a tendency to put her nose in places she shouldn't and she's already on thin ice with the council."

"June knows that she isn't supposed to be nosing around but since they asked me to join them, I have an obligation." Oscar was doing his sweet talk to Constance and she always fell for it. "So your job here is to make sure June stays out of trouble?" he clarified.

"Yes." Constance chin flew up and then down. "Since she had those nightmares, we want to make sure you two had extra protection while away. Mr. Victor thinks we are a cleaning and work crew set up by the police from a little spell we gave him."

Keep me out of trouble? I looked between them. That was far from what Patience had told me, but I kept my mouth shut. Maybe Constance was just playing along to appease Oscar. That had to be it.

"Glad we are on the same page." Oscar confirmed.

"I'd like some syrup." I held my plate of French toast out and smiled. "And you owe me an apology." I looked at Oscar.

"June, I love you. I tell you every time to keep out of these investigations, but you never listen. We are not in the safety of Whispering Falls." He tilted his head slightly to the right. "Granted, now that the Karimas are here and him too." He jabbed his finger toward Mr. Prince Charming. "Plus Madame Torres, I think you have plenty to occupy your time while I help out Teabody and the crew."

"Fine. I'll lay on the beach by myself and enjoy our honeymoon by myself." I pouted because this was the last way I wanted to spend my honeymoon. Alone.

"Hello, there," Mr. Victor's voice boomed. "Not to fear, you will not enjoy this honeymoon on your own. I have planned a private dinner for you two at the Loop, the most beautiful spot on the island for the most breathtaking sunset you will ever experience."

"That's wonderful." The excitement started to build for a romantic night with Oscar, which left me alone during the day to look in on a few things Patience and I had talked about while he thought I'd be at the beach working on a tan.

"And for you, while he is working with Officer Teabody," Mr. Victor clapped his hands and Gene came running. "Gene is going to take your breakfast and you to the spa where you are going to get the most wonderful Ayurvedic beauty treatment that will rejuvenate you from any and all stress."

Gene reached over and took my plate of French toast. Cautiously I looked at him.

"Please follow me," he said in a relaxing voice.

"Relax. Go have fun and let me do all the work." Oscar encouraged me to go with a simple kiss on the lips. "I'll see you tonight at the Loop."

I followed Gene out of the breakfast area, but not without Mr. Prince Charming darting in and out of the palm trees. I had noticed that when Mr. Victor and Gene had come around, he made himself pretty much invisible.

The spa was a little walk from the other areas of the island. It was completely secluded and overlooked the sea along with a beautiful tranquility garden of lush island plants. The treatment room was a bohio room with a table covered in white linens. Just outside the room was in infinity pool big enough for two that overlooked the bay. Mr. Victor said the Loop had the most spectacular view of the sunset, and I would say the spa had the most spectacular view of the ocean. The greens and blues of the deep sea were exaggerated from the view and miles upon miles of the blue skies extended out in front of me.

"If you wouldn't mind, you can take your clothes off and cleanse yourself in the infinity pool. Take your robe with you so you can easily slip into the sheets on the table when you return for your treatment." Gene had his hands clasped in front of him.

"Thank you." I seized the moment. "I'm assuming you grew up around here?" Suddenly it occurred to me that I had no idea who these people were.

"I'm here to serve you, not discuss my past." He led me back into the bohio room and pointed me to the white linen chair where there was a white robe draped over the arm.

"After you change your clothes, you can get into the cleansing pool until your massage therapist comes to give you your massage." Gene didn't look me in the eyes. His head was drawn down. His fingers fiddled together.

"Thanks, Gene." I inhaled deeply knowing that Gene had been well versed in what he was supposed to say to the guests if he was asked about his life.

I wasn't about to get into the cleansing pool without my clothes on. Even though Gene said that no one could see me and I was alone, I still wasn't comfortable. I sat down on the edge and put my toes in. I swirled them around and around in the same shape as the swirl charm Mr. Prince Charming had given me.

The images of Patrick on the beach and the images from my nightmare slid through my brain. There were some similarities and some differences. His eyes in my nightmare were not the same eyes as in real life. The diamond gemmed eyes lit up in the nightmare and I could only think it was due to me needing it to light up the dark ocean for me to see him. But the orange swirl was not in the real life version. Was that just to give me the security of the meaning of the charm since they were the same shape?

Gently I tapped the surface of the water with my toe and watched as the ripples got bigger and bigger.

Then there was the red hair Officer Teabody told Oscar about. The only person on the island that had red hair was Violet, who did have a past with him. Maybe not a big past, but enough of one that made her fall in love with him. I know for sure that I heard him say he loved her. Or did he mean he loved Juliette?

A light musical song played in the distance and brought me out of my sleuthing. I could feel my shoulders get more tense when I thought about the murder. Oscar was right. I needed to enjoy the spa and let him do his job. I had Patience and Mr. Prince Charming as well as Madame Torres if I needed someone or something.

"Are you ready?" the soft-spoken voice asked from the other side of the curtains.

I laid on the table with my head facing down in the doughnut with my body wrapped up like a burrito.

"I'm ready," I confirmed.

My eyes darted back and forth when I heard the shuffling of feet come into the room.

"We only use the Indian practice of Ayurveda. It is one of the world's oldest holistic healing systems. It was developed thousands of years ago in India." The woman told me something I already knew. I let her continue to tell me all about it and how it was going to rejuvenate my body along with the cleansing spa. "But you know all about that, right June?"

"Patience?" Her old woman, thick-soled white shoes came into focus as she let the hot oil treatment drip over my body from the urn that was used in Ayurveda treatments. "You are also the massage therapist?"

"I'm doing it all." She sighed. "Sister said that Oscar was asking all sorts of questions when you were at the breakfast buffet."

"Does Constance know that you and I are working together?" I asked, already knowing her answer by her stalling. I jumped up. I'd gathered the extra material in my fist and held it close to my chest. "You mean to tell me that you really were sent here just to make sure I didn't get myself in trouble and you and I are investigating on our own?"

"It sounded like a lot of fun when you assumed that this morning," she muttered uneasily and took a step back, her hands dripping with oil. "I want to help. I never get to do anything but roll in dead bodies, and roll them out. Sister always gets to have all the fun."

I bit the corner of my lips and thought for a second. Oscar wouldn't approve and I probably shouldn't involve her. But there were plenty of times I'd gotten my nose into something I shouldn't have.

"Fine." I got off the table and got nose-to-nose with her. "If you breathe a word of this to your sister or anyone else, like Oscar, then we are done. Through."

"Okay." Her eyes filled with excitement. She bounced on the balls of her feet. "What do I need to do?"

"Well, it seems that Patrick has been keeping a secret love affair with Violet all these years." I knew what I was about to say was a big assumption, but I had to start somewhere. "I heard them talking with my own ears. I heard Patrick tell her that he loved her."

"Really?" She rubbed her hands together before she put her finger in the air and walked back and forth in front of the curtains that were blowing in the sea's breeze. "You think that Mr. Victor killed Patrick because Patrick wronged his daughter."

I pondered what she'd said for a minute or two while she continued to walk around the room. The wind caused the curtain to fly over Patience's head. What she was suggesting was a good thought. I never even thought that Mr. Victor might be upset with Patrick for breaking Violet's heart.

I knew I could talk to Violet in a girly way and get some answers. But Mr. Victor was altogether a different nut to crack. He was definitely someone to look into.

"Pweft, pweft." Her lips flapped.

"Well, no." Incomplete thoughts swirled through my head. "I wasn't thinking Mr. Victor had anything to do with it. But I guess we can look at him."

"You are thinking Violet killed him because he showed up here with Juliette. And all this time since Patrick's last visit, Violet thought he was thinking of her like she was of him. When in reality he was home meeting Juliette, falling in love, and had picked someone else." Her voice trailed off. There was a distant look in her eye.

"Are you okay?" I asked.

"I'm fine." She snapped back out of her head. She shuffled over. "Just wondered what sister was doing."

"Are you going to be able to focus enough to help me?"

"Um. . no. . .I mean yes." Her fingers fiddled before she used them to push her glasses back up on her nose. She shook her head. "Yes."

"Okay." In the excitement, I had almost forgotten that I was working with Patience Karima of all the spiritualists to work with. "All I need you to do is get me the keys to Mr. Victor's office."

"How do I do that?" she asked.

"I thought you said that he thinks you are here as the maid service according to the Elders." I waved my hand in the air, circling it at the wrist.

She looked confused.

"You and Constance were sent here to help keep me safe by the Order of Elders, right." I said between gritted teeth.

"Oh yes. That." She nodded and smiled. "Keep June out of trouble. Yes."

"Just try to get me a key to somewhere he goes. Office. His room. Anywhere." At this point I knew that she wasn't going to be as big of a help to me as I had wanted, but I had to work with the hand I was dealt. In this case. . .Patience Karima was going to have to be my sidekick.

Chapter Ten

"Good evening, June," Mr. Victor stood at the entrance of our villa. Still in his white suit. His voice made my skin crawl now that I had him on my short list of suspects in the murder of Patrick.

In my head, I had spent the afternoon looking out into the ocean and putting together a very valid reason for him to have killed Patrick. Everything came back around to him being upset with Patrick for breaking his daughter's heart.

"Your chariot awaits you." He peeled back the curtains.

There was a twilight carriage and white horse just like I would imagine Cinderella having, waiting for me with one handsome Oscar Park inside. Dressed in a white suit just like Mr. Victor's.

"Thank you." I ran my hand down my black hair and continued down to the black spaghetti-strapped dress I had picked out for our romantic dinner.

I grabbed my bag and clutched it in one hand while Mr. Victor offered to help me up with my other hand.

"No thank you." I politely left out *you murderer*.

"June," Oscar scolded me like I was a little girl.

"I want you to help me." I made up for my lack of manners.

"Very good." Mr. Victor laughed. "Your groom may help you."

Oscar got out of the carriage and gently helped me up.

"Have a wonderful evening." Mr. Victor waved to us as the horse took off on its own slow and steady pace.

"No driver?" I asked and looked back over my shoulder at Mr. Victor. He was still waving and smiling. There was no man on this Earth as happy as he was pretending to be. He wasn't even that happy.

Murderer.

"No. Just me and you. The horse knows where to go." Oscar gathered me into his arms and held me snugly. "This is exactly what I need." A sigh escaped his lips.

I looked up into his big blue eyes. The same eyes that were relaxed yesterday before this whole mess happened were now back to the same eyes that had left Whispering Falls. Filled with worry. Fear. Anxiety.

I parted my lips and raised myself to meet his kiss. Memories of our wedding night were pure and clear as if it had just happened. As his kiss deepened, the passion rose up in me like the hottest fire, clouding my brain of anything I really wanted to tell him.

I closed my eyes and let myself get lost in his kiss before I leaned into him and settled in for the ride to the Loop. His broad chest heaved up and down with each breath he took. And each release was longer than the last as the stress melted from his body. So many times I had watched him after his long days at work decompress and become the Oscar I had married. The man of my dreams.

The horse climbed the island terrain. The path was big enough for the carriage and the sides dropped off like a cliff. The lights from the beach grew smaller and smaller as the horse pulled the carriage higher and higher.

The moon was out but the stars had yet to dot the black midnight sky for miles. Oscar's arms were warm around me as the salty breeze nipped at my bare arms.

When the horse stopped, Gene was waiting with a cheese platter, vegetable tray, fruit plate, and a bottle of wine with two glasses sitting on a blanket with lit tiki-torches overlooking the sea.

"Good evening, Mr. and Mrs. Park." Gene bowed down in respect. "The sun will be setting within the next twenty minutes. After that we will be here to pick you up in a couple of hours. You are welcome to do whatever it is you like. No one can see you or hear you unless you call from the phone." He blushed when he looked at us.

Oscar had a big grin on his face. I knew what he wanted to do, but I wanted to talk to him about Mr. Victor and why I thought he should be looked at as the killer along with Violet.

"We will be back in a few hours to pick you up," Gene said after Oscar helped me out of the carriage.

Gene got in the carriage and he and the horse moseyed back the way we'd come up, leaving us to do whatever it was our hearts desired.

"What on Earth are we going to do with all of this?" Oscar spread his arms out wide in front of us. It was the most spectacular view. The light blue water looked peaceful, not like the churning the night before as it gulped up the life of Patrick. "Especially when the sun sets." He pulled me close, giving me a never-to-forget kiss that made my toes curl.

We sat down on the blanket. Oscar handed me a glass of wine.

"To us." The glasses clinked and we both took a sip. Even with everything going on, I was blissfully happy. I felt fully alive when I was with Oscar.

"To us," I repeated, taking another sip.

"There you are," the exasperated voice called from behind us. "It took us forever to get up here."

Patience Karima had sweat dripping down her face. Her housecoat was unzipped to the top of her bosoms. Mr.

Prince Charming trailed alongside her with his tail dancing in the air. I swear he had a grin on his face.

"Shoooweee." She stuck her hand in her bra and pulled out a tissue. She wiped her face and then fanned herself with it. She offered it to Mr. Prince Charming. "You need a dab."

Mr. Prince Charming batted it away.

"I'm telling you." She plopped down next to Oscar and grabbed one of the vines of grapes. She huffed and puffed, "It took me a minute, but I did it."

She plucked a big round grape off the vine and threw it in her mouth.

She stuck her hand in her bra again and pulled out a key. She held it up.

"Got it." She grabbed the wine glass out of Oscar's hand. "You don't mind do you? I'm thirsty." She tipped the glass all the way up in the air and let the liquid fill her mouth. *Pweft, pweft.* Wine shot out of her mouth like a fountain and all over Oscar's face. "That's not grape juice." Her nose curled in disgust.

Oscar's brow pulled into an affronted frown and he jumped up. He didn't look back at us before he started to stalk toward the path.

"Before you go and get mad," I scurried toward an angry Oscar. "Hear me out."

He stopped and turned.

His mouth shifted open, he closed his eyes and slowly shook his head back and forth.

"I'm not so sure Violet killed Patrick." I talked fast in order to save what little marriage I suddenly had.

"Don't you think I already know that? Tell me something I don't know." His head shaking got faster. He ran his hand through his hair. "I can't believe this."

"Patrick's family has been coming here for years. He and Violet were lovers. I would bet anything on it." It was not confirmed, but there had to be more than just a friendship.

"What does that mean?" Oscar seemed to be interested now.

"I'm just saying, let me talk to Violet and see what her real history is with Patrick." I shrugged. "I can give her some girl time that I'm sure she craves since she never gets any and I'm sure I can pull the history of Patrick out of her."

I put my hand on his arm.

"The evidence is the evidence." He thrust away from me. Disappointment sat on his face. I'd broken the promise and he knew it. "Do you think Mr. Victor would plant his daughter's own hair under Patrick's fingernails if he loved her so much?"

"Well," It was something I hadn't thought of. "No. But. . ." I snapped. "But Juliette would."

"Now you have lost your mind. And she isn't helping." He pointed to Patience. "I'm going to get in contact with the Order of Elders and see if you can go home while I stay here until Patrick's murder is solved." His eyes stabbed me. "The old-fashioned police way. And the key?" Oscar looked over at Patience. "What is that?"

"I asked her to get me the key to Mr. Victor's living quarters or office so I could take a little look around." I knew Oscar would never go for it. *It's not going to hurt me looking around. Me and you are a team, in or out of Whispering Falls,* I thought.

I pointed to him and before I knew what I was doing, lightning shot from the tip of my finger and my thoughts became a reality. I jerked my finger back and curled it in my palm. I'd completely forgotten about that darn finger spell.

"I know we are a team and yes, you can look around. Just don't get hurt," he was agreeable.

Patience's mouth dropped. Her eyes darted between me and my finger. I curled it in my palm and put my hand behind my back.

Oscar sat on the blanket and grabbed cheese and a cracker before pouring him some more wine.

"It's pretty, isn't it." He lifted his chin and looked over the scenery.

"Since when could you do that?" Patience asked in a whisper. She bent down and looked at my finger. "That is one trick I've never seen you use."

"It's temporary." My mind reeled with how I could cover up my big boo-boo. Not only had I put a spell on Oscar to agree with what my mind was thinking, I had also let Patience Karima see me do it. A big no-no according to Aunt Helena. "And a big secret. Understand?"

"Understand." Patience couldn't take her eyes off my finger.

"Crap." I glanced over her shoulder, the sun had already set and Oscar was chowing down on the fruit and cheese.

Chapter Eleven

"Good morning." Oscar was in a chipper mood. He bent down and kissed my head.

He was already dressed and had a cup of coffee on the bedside table next to me.

"Last night was amazing at the Loop." He stood next to the bed and glanced out over the ocean. "Just look at this place." There was an infectious smile on his face.

I turned over on my belly and looked out at the view.

"Who on Earth ever thought of putting a hotel room in the middle of the ocean?" he asked. "So." He turned back to me. "You are going to go and look around Mr. Victor's office to see what the history of Patrick's family has been?"

I never thought of that, but it was a good idea.

"And you need to find out where exactly he sent Violet yesterday. So talking to her would be a great idea." He was so agreeable.

I continued to look out at the calm blue sea while I rubbed my fingers together. Too bad the spell was only temporary because I was enjoying agreeable cop Oscar.

"I've got it covered." I rolled back over. Mr. Prince Charming was lying at the end of the bed curled up in a little ball. "I'll be safe."

"You better be." He ran his hand over my bedhead before dipping his lips to give me a kiss on the top of my head. "I've got to go meet Officer Teabody at the lodge."

"Okay." I sat up and reached out to pet my ornery familiar who didn't seem to be too worried about my safety.

Meow. He finally moved after Oscar had walked across the bridge and was walking down the beach toward the lodge. He walked over to the table and sat next to Madame Torres. Her face floated inside the glass ball. Both of them watching as Oscar kicked up the surf on his way to meet Officer Teabody.

"It's a shame that we haven't really been able to enjoy our honeymoon." I frowned recalling how excited we were to live somewhat of a normal life for the next few days.

"You will." Madame Torres bounced around inside her ball. Her eyes blinked. Her lids were painted in yellow. Her dark lashes drew up when she opened her lids. The red rouge on the balls of her cheeks matched her lipstick. "It will come when it will come." She winked. Her face was replaced with a large diamond.

Her words were so simple but held so much more meaning. My eyes narrowed when I noticed the floating gem. Mr. Prince Charming smacked the glass ball with his paw and Madame Torres went black.

There was no time to spare and I needed to help out in any way that I could. I reached over and grabbed the flip phone. I opened it and waited to see what would happen.

"Can I help you, June?" Gene's young voice asked.

"I'm looking for Violet. Is she there?" I asked.

"Yes, ma'am." He clicked off. I waited for him to click back on the phone but instead there was a knock coming from the front of the room. There was a shadowy figure on the other side of the flowing curtain.

"Did you ask for me?" Violet asked.

"Please come in." I got out of bed and grabbed my bathing suit before I headed straight to the bathroom. "I'm going to get my suit on and I'll be right out."

I heard her walk into the villa. There wasn't any more movement. When I walked out of the bathroom, she was standing near my suitcase. My potion bottles were on top of my clothes where I had left them.

"I wanted to ask how you were doing." I noticed the bags under her eyes were dark and sagging. "I know that it has to be lonely here with no girlfriends to talk to."

Her broken voice was a mere whisper. "I know you saw us talking yesterday."

"That was you?" I asked, pretending that I didn't know.

"I've known Patrick since we were children. His family came here for their vacations initially, later it was for Peter. He loves the sand and beach, so they started to spend summers here." A tear trickled down her cheek. "After we started to get older, our attraction for one another grew and he was and is the only man I have ever made love to."

I gulped.

"While he was off to college, I was here. My father insisted I learn how to run the island and that I didn't need a college education when I told him I wanted to go to the states to be with Patrick. Father was beside himself. Neither his parents nor my father knew we had the intimate relationship we did until I told my father about my love for Patrick." Another tear trickled, but I wasn't falling for the murderess sympathy card. "His parents still continued to come with Peter. They would go on all day excursions because Patrick's father was always on the hunt for a diamond mine."

"Diamond mine?" My gut tickled. My intuition set a big alarm off. Madame Torres was trying to tell me something. I was going to have to get better at reading her.

"Yes." She turned toward the bay and continued to tell me her tale, "They own P&P Jewels."

"As in the national chain?" I asked remembering how I would stand in front of the P&P Jewels window admiring the charm bracelets on display. I had wanted a charm bracelet so badly. Oscar knew it. So when Mr. Prince Charming had shown up with the small turtle charm hooked onto his dingy collar, Oscar had given me his mom's old bracelet to attach the charm.

P&P Jewels was everywhere. And their commercials too.

"Patrick and Peter." She smiled and brought her hands up to her ears where she played with a diamond stud earring. "Patrick gave these to me the last time we made love."

"When was that?" I asked.

"A year ago, after his parents died. Peter was having a hard time so Patrick brought him here." Violet turned to me. "Patrick had slipped away with me for a few hours. He even told me he loved me. We made love and he promised he'd be back. It was the last time I'd seen him until he showed up yesterday with her."

"Was he with Juliette a year ago?" I asked.

"I don't know. He didn't mention her." She blinked back more tears.

"And she's why you killed him?" It seemed like a fair question.

"Killed him?" The look of disgust clouded her face. "You think I killed him? Why on Earth would I do that?"

"Scorned woman would probably be at the top of the list." I rubbed my finger and thumb together to be ready just in case I needed a little help. "You couldn't stand seeing him with her. Plus I'm now sure that the drinks you accidentally spilled on her was far from accidental."

"It was an accident." She shied away. "I had lost all sense of myself when I saw it was Patrick and her together.

Father had told me we had a wedding party, which wasn't unusual for the island. Conveniently, he left out that it was Patrick and her."

She sat down on the chair and hung her head. It was second nature for me to try to comfort anyone in distress. I laid a hand on her. Instantly my intuition told me that she was broken inside. She was doing everything she could to keep it together. But my intuition didn't tell me if she was guilty.

"Let me get you some water." I walked over to the water bottles on the table next to my suitcase and slipped the potion bottle out of my bag.

Violet's head was still in her hands as she mourned the death of her one and only true love. Lightly I tapped a couple drips from the potion bottle and used my finger to stir it. Since I didn't have all of my heartbreak potion ingredients with me, I tapped into Violet's ache and summoned my newfound finger gift to do the magic for me. A bolt of lightning surged out of the tip of my finger and into the glass, creating its own perfect storm of healing a heartache.

"Here." I handed her the glass. "Drink all of it so you can be hydrated."

She took the glass. Tears glistened on her heart-shaped face. She almost looked angelic. I believed what she had said but could she really kill the man she loved?

"I have to tell you that Patrick had red hair stuck under his nails and was gripping some red hair as well." I knew that if she couldn't explain why, that was she was going to be Oscar's number one suspect. No matter how much I would tell him that she wasn't the killer, he went by the hard evidence.

"I'm not sure why." She shook her head and held the glass with both hands to try to steady her trembling. "I took them night diving because my father insisted. I dropped them off at the dock and they went on their way."

"What did he say to you yesterday when I saw the two of you at the trees?" I wanted to hear it all. Things that might not be clues to her sometimes were the biggest clues of the case.

"He told me he had written me a few times and they came back as return to sender. He even said that he'd told me about him and Juliette falling in love. Something he never expected. He was happy that his parents had gotten to meet her before they died." She took another drink. She licked her lips and continued, "I reminded him of our promises to each other and he said that he had Peter to think about and at one time living on the island was perfect for Peter, but now Peter was doing so much better that he wouldn't have to sell the business and move here. I told him he could move his headquarters here, but he insisted he couldn't."

"He was willing to sell the business?" That seemed strange.

"He wasn't into the diamond mines and he only did what his parents wanted him to do." She paused for a second. "Like I did with my father. My father saw Patrick leave my villa last night and told me if I didn't stop Patrick from contacting me, he would. I told my father I couldn't promise anything and I was going to crash the wedding. Father sent me to the mainland."

"So that is where you were yesterday?" I asked.

"He sent me to the textile store to pick up more fabrics." She folded her hands in her lap.

"So this," I pulled the hanky Patrick had given me out of my bag, "was made by you?"

She took it from my hands. A smile curved on her lips and she pressed the hanky to her cheek. Her eyes closed and she inhaled through her nose.

"It smells like him," she whispered. "Now he's dead."

She downed the rest of the water and then stood up.

"I've taken enough of your time." She set the glass down on the table. "You don't need to worry about my problems. Enjoy your honeymoon. My father would die if he knew I told you all of this."

"Don't worry." I reached and grabbed her hands, giving them a light squeeze. "Your secrets are safe with me. I just want you to feel better. And know that I'm so sorry you had to go through all this."

"What was it that you needed to see me for?" she asked.

"Nothing. I wanted to give you this." With my back turned, I dug deep into my suitcase until I felt another sunscreen bottle. With my grip around the bottle, I closed my eyes and pictured Violet on the beach, her red hair, her freckles, the sand and the sun. I tapped the bottle with my finger and let the magic transfer to the bottle, sending the perfect SPF into the bottle for her.

"I think this will work wonders for your skin tone." I turned around and held the bottle out. "It's a little too much SPF for me, so I thought you could use it."

"Thanks. I have to go." She forced a grin and took the bottle. "My father is making me groom the horse this morning while he meets with Teabody. He wants me out of sight. I appreciate your kindness, June."

As she walked out of the room, the curtain separating the outside world blew in with a breeze.

Chapter Twelve

"What was that about?" Patience appeared on the bridge leading over the water to the villa. Her hands gripped the rope sides and each one of her steps was taken with caution. The bridge swayed back and forth. Little noises of fright escaped her lips.

"I'm not wasting any time. I wanted to talk to her about why she left the island." I contemplated what she'd said about her father and how he didn't like hearing of her relationship with Patrick.

"It does make her look awfully suspicious." Patience amazed me. Sometimes she was so level headed and reasonable and other times not so much.

"Her father sent her to the mainland." I grabbed my bag and flung it across my body. "Sitting in here all day isn't going to help solve anything."

I ran my hand down my bag. The key I'd gotten from Patience last night at the Loop was still in there.

"Now what?" Patience sounded defeated.

"We go look in Mr. Victor's office." I patted my bag.

"I can't." Her brows dipped. "I've got to clean some villas."

"Well, Mr. Victor is gone to meet with the police which gives me access to the offices without having to worry about him being there." I had a niggling suspicion I was going to find something very important. My gut told me I had to go and go now.

Rowl! Rowl! Mr. Prince Charming jumped up on his hind legs and scratched my bare wrist.

"My bracelet." I hurried back over to the bedside table where I'd taken off my bracelet and clasped it back on.

When I turned back around, Patience was gone and the bridge was swinging back and forth over the water.

"Ready?" I asked Mr. Prince Charming. He swayed his tail in the air and danced his way across the bridge.

Before I followed him, I grabbed Madame Torres and stuck her in the bottom of my bag.

"No way," she protested. "I thought these days were over. Long over."

"I might need you." I ignored her griping and headed out.

Instead of taking the beach all the way to the lodge, Mr. Prince Charming decided we would take the path that Gene had taken us on the first day we'd gotten there. It was a direct path to the lodge and there was no time to waste.

"You have to tell me what you did with it, Peter." The voice was stern and belonged to Juliette. Between the palm trees, I could see that Juliette and Peter were sitting in the hammock.

"It's Patrick's and you can't keep it," Juliette said with a bite.

"Mine." Peter's voice was matter-of-fact. He had a grip on the chocolate milk bottle in his hand. "All mine. Daddy said."

"But we are family now." Juliette's voice had turned gentle, almost mothering. "I'm going to take care of you. When we get home, I'll take you to the water park. We can even go to the zoo and ride the train like you love to do. Please. Please give it back to me."

A limb crunched under my step and Juliette's head shot up. She looked at me with a savage fire. I stepped off the path and over a few fallen coconuts on my way over to them. The sun glistened in dots all over the sand and looked like the diamonds Madame Torres had floating in her glass ball.

"Good morning, June." She forced a slight wave.

"How are you?" I stopped just shy of the hammock. Peter looked up at me. His eyes were red and his cheeks were tear stained.

"I'm fine." She lifted her hand and rubbed Peter's back. He jerked away from her. "Peter is having a hard time and I think it's best we leave."

"No. I want to stay. Find the treasure like my dad. Like my Patrick." Peter pouted.

"All the people from my wedding talked to the police and decided to head back to the states. Unfortunately, if I can't get Peter to agree to go and have to force him, he has to get sedated and I just don't want to do that." Her voice cracked. A tear fell from the corner of her eye. "Patrick never drugged Peter and now I'm all he has."

"There is no other true family?" I asked. My heart broke for Peter.

"No. That's why we were getting guardianship." She frowned. "Now the guardianship goes to me." She stood up. Peter took the opportunity to lie all the way down on the hammock.

She nodded for me to follow her.

"I don't know how much more I can take," she sobbed when we were a good distance away from Peter. She looked over my shoulder at him. "I love Peter, but I don't know how to care for a grown man with special needs. I just followed Patrick's lead. For the past year, Patrick has been holding down the business while I answered the phones for him after I'd drop Peter off at daycare."

"You've done all you can do." I knew my words wouldn't comfort her, but I wasn't sure what else to say. "When my dad died, I was young. But when my mom died it devastated me. It took me a long time to heal and I don't have the issues that Peter has." I ran my hand down her arm and squeezed her hand. "You have to have time to heal yourself. I'm sure it's best for Peter to get back to his normal routine at home, so if you have to sedate him to get him home, it's probably for the best."

"Poor kid has had a black cloud following him for a year." The sunlight hit her face perfectly, causing the tears to glisten like the diamonds.

This was about the fourth time the diamonds from my nightmare had popped up. My intuition was on high alert.

"What do you mean by black cloud?" I asked.

"First the only safe place he truly had, his home, burned down. His parents, who he knew kept him safe and secure, died. Don't get me wrong." She shuffled her feet and reached over to pick off a piece of the palm tree. "Patrick and Peter have," she paused, "had, had a great time together. But Patrick didn't want to be a dad or caregiver. We had our whole life in front of us. Now." Her head dropped and bounced up and down as the sobs came again. "Not only do I have to come to grips that the love of my life has been killed, but now I'm the caregiver to Peter."

I curled my arms around her and drew her into a hug.

"I'm so sorry." I patted her back as she used my shoulder to cry on. "You are a strong woman that will be able to get through this. I'm sure Patrick had a plan and you know the plan. You are just going to have to execute the plan without him. Make his wishes come true."

The warmth of the potion bottle in my bag warmed against my belly. My intuition told me that I needed to help her and Peter.

"You said he's had a black cloud. You can bring him sunny skies." I pulled away from her.

She wiped her tears with the palm of her hand. She forced a smile. The corners of her sad eyes dipped down. She nodded. The smile turned into a frown.

"You're right." She licked her lips. "I'm so thirsty."

"Why don't we get Peter and go have a drink in the lodge." If I could get her in the lodge and seated with Peter, I could get a little potion in there to help them both and still have time to go into Mr. Victor's office to look around. But time was wasting away.

"What is that?" Her eyes shot over my shoulder. "Get away from him!" She pushed past me.

Mr. Prince Charming had jumped up in Peter's lap and was dragging his tail underneath Peter's chin causing Peter to laugh and giggle. Mr. Prince Charming stuck his long tongue down the chocolate milk bottle and lapped up a big drink.

"Get!" she screamed and flailed toward my cat who scurried off.

"No!" Peter got out of the hammock and thrust his fists down to the ground. The bottle flung to the ground and chocolate milk sprayed everywhere. "Kitty, kitty!" He ran in the direction where Mr. Prince Charming had run.

"Peter stop!" Juliette ran after him. "June, I'll have to take a rain check on getting a drink!"

Juliette, Peter and Mr. Prince Charming ran after each other leaving me standing there. I looked at the lodge, and then back at them. Mr. Prince Charming could take care of himself. I had a feeling Peter could take better care of himself than Juliette could take care of herself.

My gut tugged. While I had the opportunity, I knew I had to go in the offices and find what my intuition was leading me to find.

Chapter Thirteen

The halls of the lodge were lit up by the sun streaming down the open hall. I looked at the photos down the hall a little closer than the first time Gene had showed us the office area. The first photo had to have been when Mr. Victor had first moved to the island. He was standing in front of the lodge with a small, pig-tailed, freckled-face redhead propped up on his shoulder. She was smiling ear-to-ear with a key dangling from her fingers. The same key that Patience had given me.

The next picture was the two of them with their first resort patrons. They both had on the same white suits only in smaller sizes. As the pictures progressed, so did their ages. The one thing I noticed was there was no other woman in the photos, no mother figure. Only women on vacations with their family. There was another photo of a young Violet sitting on the beach with a little boy. By the almond shape of the boy's eyes, I could tell it was Patrick. I followed the photos until I found every single photo that Patrick was in.

There were a total of five photos in all. I wasn't sure of the years or how old they were, but they'd gotten older as the photos had progressed. In the photo where Violet had taken on some puberty weight, was when Patrick had disappeared from the island photos. A couple of photos later, there was a picture of three people alongside a thinner Violet. One of them was Peter and the older couple who I assumed to be their parents. But no Patrick. My gut told me it was when Patrick was off to college because Violet still looked young, but her body had turned to that of a woman. Her breasts were bigger; her hips were more rounded.

Suddenly on the other side of the wall was when Gene had shown up. I wondered where he'd come from.

The answers had to be buried on this island somewhere. I sighed. Maybe Peter was right. But instead of treasure being buried on the island, it was the secrets that needed to be uncovered.

I took the key out of my bag and tried it in the door with Mr. Victor's name on it. When it unlocked and I was inside, I was happy to see that Patience had done exactly what I'd asked her to do. Relief settled in my gut as I dug down in my bag and pulled out Madame Torres.

"Uncover the secrets held deep within the murder." I put the key on the desk and ran my hand in a circular motion over her.

The insides of my familiar curled into a swirl of a vicious tornado. The rage and anger swelled up inside of her. Specks of white and orange bubbled up, sending the funnel cloud into a calm swirl.

The water cleared and a document floated, magnified by the glass. I touched the ball and the document expanded. The word adoption appeared in bold red letters followed up by a photo of a safe.

"Where is the safe?" I asked and looked around the room.

The room was made of teak wood. The desk was just a top with four legs that sat on a concrete floor over a woven rug. There wasn't a file cabinet or any furniture other than that. The bamboo fan ticked in the silence.

The sound of footsteps came from the other side of the door and the handle turned. I grabbed Madame Torres and threw her in my bag. My hand grazed one of the books Ophelia had given me and I pulled it out. I sat on the floor cross-legged in front of the desk and looked at the book as if I were reading it while I waited for Mr. Victor to come back.

When Mr. Victor opened the door a strange cold expression was on his face.

"Ms. Heal." He stopped.

My whole body tensed. My heart thumped against my rib cage.

He looked around. He swung the door and looked behind it.

"Are you needing something?" he asked and swept across the floor, sitting in the chair behind the desk.

I looked down at the book—it just so happened to be the myths and legends book Ophelia had given me.

"I was looking through this book about Tulip Island and wondered if the legend was true." I waved the book in the air and rolled my eyes, playing off the false ideas of myths.

"Which myth would that be?" His brows rose.

"Um…" I glanced down at the book. "Buried treasure," I read the headline.

A thunderbolt jagged through me. It was as though Ophelia had given me this book because she knew I was going to need it. My intuition went off like an alarm. Peter's hand-drawn map was of treasure.

"Oh, June." Mr. Victor threw his head back. A raspy chuckle escaped him. "You have a very active imagination and so does that book." He gestured toward the book. "Ever since that book was published, Tulip Island has been flooded with people wanting to find this mysterious buried treasure."

I gulped.

"Well, I was just thinking that maybe Patrick knew something about the treasure." I shrugged. I put my book back in the bag and pushed myself up to standing. "But I guess you are right. I have a very active imagination."

"I understand this has been a very stressful honeymoon." He stood back up. His eyes hooded like a hawk. "Let me give you and Mr. Park a free week after all of this nonsense clears so you can enjoy the island fully."

"Would you throw in a trip to the volcano?" There was no way I was ever going to come back to Tulip Island. Throwing in the ever-so-off-limits volcano was just my gut wanting to see his reaction.

"We'd be more than happy to throw in a trip to the volcano, but you can't sue me if it. . ." He smacked his hands in the air. "Explodes," the sarcasm dripped from his mouth.

"Thank you." I scurried out of the office and back down the hall to the dining area.

Oscar and Officer Teabody were talking to Gene at a table next to the buffet. I slipped out without Oscar seeing me and planted myself in a beach chair. I knew better than to think that Ophelia had just-so-happened to throw in a book about myths and legends.

Chapter Fourteen

Figuring out what Madame Torres was trying to tell me about the adoption paper was last on my mind and I figured Mr. Victor had adopted Violet and Gene. There could be no other explanation to what was going on.

Apparently Juliette and Peter had put their differences aside. They were in the ocean. Peter was flipping and flopping with his snorkel gear on. He looked like a whale when he came up for air and shot the water out of the snorkel tube. Juliette held the shell bag as he put his treasures in it.

The waves were larger and seemed to be crashing with anger as they hit the shore. Over the roar of the sea, I could hear Juliette encouraging him to find more. Praising him for the good job he was doing. In all hopes of hope, she might've listened to my encouragement before my pesky cat had decided to drink from chocolate milk jug.

Mewl. The ornery cat appeared next to me. His tail dragged along the beach chair before he disappeared under it.

"You naughty cat." I shut the book and sat on the edge of the chair. "You know you aren't supposed to drink milk, much less chocolate."

Mewl. He threw his leg up in the air. Sand went flying. He ignored it and began to clean himself.

For now I was safe. He was with me. It was also a good time to sneak into Peter's villa and give him a little spell that I knew could help him get on a plane and get home safely. It was for the good of him and to help him move on with his life. Juliette was going to take care of him and that's what mattered.

I quickly gathered my things before Juliette saw me and headed back toward the lodge. The path to the villas where the wedding party was staying was to the left of the lodge while we were to the right.

When I passed the lodge, Oscar and Officer Teabody were still talking to Gene so I slipped past with Mr. Prince Charming leading the way. The path looked the same as mine and Oscar's. It was sandy with palm trees on both sides shading the path. The breeze coming off the ocean had kicked up to more of a wind. I looked out beyond the path at the ocean and noticed the clouds in the distance were not like the fluffy cotton balls. They were dark with grey and black streaks.

"Good, boy." I knew the villa he'd led me straight to was Peter's and Patrick's. "Let's give Peter that spell."

Mr. Prince Charming ran over the bridge. The sea underneath was not the calm sea from earlier but was splashing up against the bridge that led over to the villa. The villa was laid out exactly like ours and I knew the extra chocolate milks had to be in the refrigerator. I was right.

I opened it and inside the door it was filled with a couple rows to last Peter a full week. I put my bag on the floor and took out Madame Torres and then the generic potion bottle. I unscrewed the milk and uncorked the potion, dripping a little bit of it into the milk bottles.

After I secured the lids, I waved my hand over the bottles.

"Rest thee mind, calm the soul, love the hands that take you home." I chanted a couple of times before I opened my eyes. The milk was bubbling inside of the bottle, which meant the potion took and I was able to help out not only Juliette, but also Peter.

Mr. Prince Charming paced back and forth between me and the villa bridge. Darkness had fallen over the ocean. The sound of the waves crashed against the shore.

"Are you okay?" I asked as I gathered my things and put the milk bottles back in the refrigerator. His tail pointed in the direction of the door. It was time for us to go. He had something on his radar.

The clash of thunder and strike of lightning hit the ocean in the distance. It lit up the villa. I steadied myself on the table next to the refrigerator and noticed Peter's drawn treasure map.

Mewl! Mewl! Mr. Prince Charming darted out of the villa. It was my cue to get out of there.

For a moment I contemplated taking the map and seeing if there was any resemblance to the references in the book. But I knew if Peter lost it, he might not leave even with the potion. I took Madame Torres out of my bag.

"Madame Torres, remember this map." I held onto the base of my crystal ball and rolled the glass over the hand-drawn map.

With no time to spare, I ran after Mr. Prince Charming. His tail was a light beacon in the dark that'd taken over the island from the tropical storm. One good thing about having a fairy-god cat was that he was able to use his keen sense to get us back to our villa using back paths before the storm had settled in on our side of the island.

The palm trees were leaning to the right with the wind thrashing through them. The thud of coconuts dropping on the ground was heard from all directions. The light was on in the villa and the storm walls had been pulled down.

"There you are!" Oscar called from the door. He held it open for us to run to safety. "Hurry before the ocean covers the bridge."

The pounding rain had started and was almost a barrier for us to run through. There wasn't a bit of blue in the sky. Angry black. The sea was angry. And the look on Oscar's face didn't seem too pleasant either.

"Now that I know that you are okay, we need to talk." He shut the door behind me. Patience and Constance Karima were sitting in chairs in the villa. The rain pounded the roof and we had to speak at a higher volume than normal.

"Ladies." I nodded.

"Your little," Patience wiggled her finger in the air, "has worn off." She referred to the agreeable spell I'd placed on Oscar last night. The one I'd done on accident.

"Shh." Constance nudged her sister. They sat next to each other with their hands clasped between their knees.

"I was under the assumption they were here to keep you safe while I did what I needed to do to get this case solved." He pointed to the two sisters. He curled his nose at Mr. Prince Charming. "He is too?"

The sisters nodded in agreement.

"Then I find out that you are in Mr. Victor's office and you had a key? A key you stole from him?" Oscar had obviously forgotten that he'd given me permission to look. "After you asked him about going to the volcano."

"He snitched on me?" I asked. I had to get the heat off of the sisters.

"He complained to the authorities that maybe we should be looking at you." Oscar ran his hands through his hair. There was displeasure in his blue eyes.

"Me?" I scoffed. "Why on Earth would I want to kill Patrick when I didn't know him?"

"I know, June. He's just trying to take the heat off of Violet." He sat on the edge of the bed. "I know the three of you and I know that you haven't left well enough alone, so spill what you know."

"You aren't going to get mad?" Constance asked.

"Not mad?" Patience repeated.

"No." Oscar's voice held authority. He was a true man of his word and I trusted him.

"I'll tell him." I put my hand up for the sisters to stop. I walked between them. "Violet confirmed to me that she and Patrick did have a love affair."

Constance gasped and put her hands over Patience's ears.

"Stop it!" Patience smacked her hands away. "He was her first lover."

Constance's mouth dropped. "June Heal." She wagged her finger at me. "You have been nothing but trouble for my sister."

"Please," I said sarcastically. "She knows way more than me."

"Yes." Patience confirmed. "Violet is in love with Patrick and he loved her. He told her so and I can't be so sure that Gene isn't their son."

"What?" Constance, Oscar and I said it at the same time. Disbelief on our faces.

"Mmmhmmmm." Patience nodded up and down. "When I was cleaning Gene's villa, he was on one of the flippy phones. He kept calling the person on the other line Mom. So I got to thinking."

"That's dangerous," Constance chirped.

"What?" I encouraged her and shushed Constance.

"I got to thinking that Violet was awfully upset over the death of a man that she'd not seen in ten years. Why hadn't he been back?" Patience tapped her temple. "Then it occurred to me that Gene is a ten-year-old boy. And those pictures frames on the wall in the lodge that I've had to dust every single day. . ."

I smacked my hands together.

"But they did see each other." I remembered Violet telling me about Patrick bringing Peter here right after their parents had died. "But he didn't mention Juliette to her. And they made love."

Patience giggled, and then turned red.

"That would explain why she'd be upset with his death." I could only imagine in Violet's mind that she and Patrick were a couple, even if the time apart was long.

Patience continued to smile. I had no time to visit the birds and the bees with her.

"There is a lull between the years though." I said, recalling how Violet had grown up really fast between a couple of the photos. "Not only that, but she'd gained weight. Baby bump." I made a circle in the front of my stomach. "Mr. Victor didn't take any photo evidence of her being pregnant and. . ." I pulled Madame Torres out of my bag. "When I went into the office."

"With the stolen key?" Oscar asked. I ignored him.

"When I went into the office, Madame Torres glowed with the word adoption. I bet Mr. Victor was going to adopt Gene or maybe Patrick's parents were going to adopt Gene."

"Either way." Oscar stood up and paced. The thunder was closer and closer. The waves were knocking up against the villa. "Patrick didn't know about Gene."

"He didn't." All the clues were coming together. "When I talked to Violet, she said that her father had intercepted all the letters that she'd written to Patrick and Patrick had written to her."

"When she saw Patrick come back to the island with Juliette, she went berserk and killed him." Patience stood up alongside us.

"We've not been able to interview her because her father sent her to the mainland so she couldn't be interviewed." Oscar rubbed his hands together.

Madame Torres lit up like the Fourth of July. Her ball glowed with lightning bolts, red flowing lava dripped from the top of the globe and settled into a raging sea. I took a step closer and looked deep within the ball.

"What is it, June?" Constance asked and stood up, looking over my shoulder. "Tell us what it is you see."

I opened my mouth when the vision came clear and I tried to speak, but nothing came out. I closed my mouth and swallowed. Hard.

"Violet." I pointed to the globe. "She's on the edge of the volcano." My eyes slid up from the globe and deep into Oscar's eyes. I uttered an inward gasp and let it come out of me. "She's getting ready to push Juliette and Peter into the hot lava."

Chapter Fifteen

Oscar did his best to get Officer Teabody on the phone. Unfortunately, the tropical storm had knocked out all the phone signals.

"Here is a map to the volcano." I grabbed the myths and legends book that Ophelia had given me out of the bag and handed it to Oscar.

"Book!" Patience cried out. She reached over and grabbed a Ding Dong off the table. She waved it in the air. "I knew I was forgetting something."

She peeled back the foil and I got a whiff. I was stressed so this called for a Ding Dong.

"I was supposed to give you the June's Gems Raven sent you." She chewed with her mouth full.

"She sent some Gems?" I asked knowing that she'd only send them if she saw something in the dough. "Where are they?"

"She ate them." Constance had sat back down and put her head in her hands. "We are in for it now. I'm going to lose my powers all because sister has gone against what the Order of Elders wanted."

"I did no such thing." Patience protested, "I have kept her safe and sound. In fact, I've helped her with this whole thing."

The two sisters argued back and forth while Oscar and I tried to figure out our next move.

"I don't like using you in this way. You are not a trained cop and this is a murder. Violet is obviously not going to stop at Patrick." His words chilled me to the bone.

"You don't have a choice unless you want Tweedledee and Tweedledum to go with you instead." I nodded toward the sisters.

"I don't like this but you're right. There is no time for the storm to clear or even get help." His icy blue eyes radiated fear. "You have got to stay behind me at all times."

"I understand." I agreed, knowing I was going to do whatever I needed to do to not only save Peter, but save Juliette.

"June, you didn't miss anything. Raven switched up the June's Gem and put some sort of red filling in it." Patience's nose snarled. She did a shimmy-shake. "Yuck. Oh and she said to read the book."

"Red filling?" Oscar asked. "Do you know what that meant?"

"Lava and the book." I rubbed my hand over the page Oscar and I were poring over. "Wait. Where is your wand?"

"We are . . .," he started to talk.

"On our honeymoon," I finished his sentence. "And if you think I believe you left your wand at home. . ."

"Alright." He stopped me. He dug his wand out of his suitcase. He held it up in the air.

Constance Karima giggled and her face turned all shades of red. She fanned herself as though she were about to faint.

"She always loved a man with a wand." Patience wiggled her brows.

"What on Earth was the Order of Elders thinking sending them here?" I turned back to him and tried to put the sisters in the back of my head. "You need to use your magic to summon the horse and carriage here. That is the only way for sure that we will get to the top of the volcano and not get lost."

Without a word, Oscar walked out of the villa in the beating rain of the tropical storm and did whatever it was he needed to do.

The sisters were too wrapped up in giggling over Oscar and how hot they thought he was to even notice me gathering all the smudge materials along with the potion bottles and the Magical Cures Book from my suitcase, shoving them into my bag.

Oscar opened the door and stuck his head in. "Let's go."

I slipped out of the villa without the sisters seeing. Mr. Prince Charming jumped on the back of the horse, which didn't flinch. We got into the carriage and I untied the plastic from around the poles and it made a clear canopy over us. I zipped up the door and then as soon as we were seated, the horse shot off in a flash.

The angry sky lit up all around us as the horse-drawn carriage climbed the trail leading to the volcano. Between the lightning bursts, I could see the red lava spit up in the air and a small trail of lava spew down the hill taking the palm trees and anything else as its victim.

Madame Torres was still not calm. Her insides churned with the angry sky and sea. Her liquid crashed so hard against her glass, I was afraid it was going to shatter. Images of the map and Peter continued to roll with the waves. She was telling me that I had to get to Peter as quick as we could.

Oscar and I sat in silence as we held on. He continued to look out of the plastic to see if we were getting any closer. The wheels of the carriage squeaked. The rush of the wind howled through the plastic and the rain pounded down like bullets from a semi-automatic.

Abruptly the horse stopped. I quickly unzipped the plastic and noticed we weren't at the top. The lava had stopped the horse.

Mr. Prince Charming jumped down. His eyes met mine and he darted off in a direction. His tail pointing the way.

"No." Oscar grabbed me as I was about to jump out. "You can't go."

I jerked away.

"If you think I've come this far to not help, you have another thing coming." I could see the dark worry that stained his crystal blue eyes. "I'll be fine."

He let go. I swiped my hand over Madame Torres and she gave us a clear picture of Violet and Juliette still on the volcano. Peter was nowhere to be found. Blood-chilling anger iced my insides thinking Violet had done something to harm Peter.

"I'll go east and you go west. We will meet in the middle on each side of Violet." Oscar grabbed my neck and pulled me to him. His lips dug deep into mine. "I love you. Be safe."

I jumped out and ran as fast as I could to find Mr. Prince Charming. He'd found a trail that led me straight up the volcano. It was a path that had already been seared from what looked like a lava flow from a long time ago. There were fresh shoeprints in the mud, which made me believe this was the path Violet, Peter and Juliette had taken to get to the top.

The rain beat into me along with the anger that only fueled me more. With every step closer to Violet I took, the images of her and Patrick kissing stirred in my head. His words haunted me. *I love you.* Then it was clear. Gene's eyes were so recognizable to me and they were the exact shape of Patrick's.

"Buried treasure." Peter rocked back and forth on the side of the trail. I barely realized it was him. He had on a hoodie sweatshirt and the hood was pulled up over his head and the strings tightly tied under his chin. Mr. Prince Charming had curled up in Peter's lap. Relief overcame me from seeing him alive that I almost wasn't able to hold back the tears.

"Hi, Peter." I bent down and spoke in a hushed whisper. I could hear some yelling coming from above but I couldn't make out what they were saying due to Mother Nature's angry turn. "You are going to be okay."

"My daddy said the treasures are in there. Diamonds for life. Diamonds for life." Peter repeated and stroked Mr. Prince Charming. There was a bottle of chocolate milk next to him and his calmness told me that the potion I had put in there had started to work.

"You stay here." I patted Mr. Prince Charming and Peter.

I swear I saw Mr. Prince Charming nodding his head right along with Peter. I rubbed my wrist and felt my charms before I stood up. I needed all the courage and protection I could muster up to even take another step.

Chapter Sixteen

As much as I wanted to clear the air with a quick light of the sage stick and dampen down the lava flow, the beating rain wasn't going to let me light it and keep it lit. Both the women were arguing and screaming at the other.

I took a step forward and the dried piece of lava rock caused me to slip, sending several more pieces down the side of the volcano with it. Violet turned. She glared at me with a burning, reproachful eye.

"June! Help me!" Juliette's desperate plea echoed.

"Don't you dare help her. She deserves what she gets." Sudden anger lit Violet's eyes. The darkness surrounded us. Red gas lifted from the volcano. The burning smell charred my nose hair.

"This is not the way to get even." I kept my voice calm and tried to reason with Violet. "You have to come down and let the authorities handle this."

"I will not sit back and let her enjoy her life after she took mine!" Violet screamed. She beat the palms of her hands on her thighs. The sky lit up with jagged bolts of lightning ending in a thunderous roar.

"He didn't want you! What can't you get through that head of yours?" Juliette screamed back. "He picked me! Me!"

"It's not him that you wanted." Violet's teeth were gritted. Her eyes narrowed. "You only wanted the diamonds. He told me. He told me that he loved me!"

Juliette moved as the lightning took another swipe at the night sky. The edges of a knife writhed under her clothing. She pulled it out and closed her hand around the knife as if somehow she was going to complete the mission.

A slight twist of her lips, she said, "He never loved you or that child you claimed was his."

"How did you know?" Violet couldn't take her eyes off the knife and neither could I. "I just told him about Gene the other day."

"Can we please go down to the lodge?" I gave one last attempt to be nice and play all mortal like.

"Shut up with your reasonable talk!" Juliette stabbed the air in front of her, blade down.

"And that's when he told me that he was getting cold feet. That's when I knew that everything I worked for over the past couple of years was going to come down to this." She pointed the tip of the knife behind her and into the volcano. "Peter!" she called. With her free hand she grabbed a copy of Peter's hand-drawn map out of her pocket. "Do you want to go get the treasure now?"

"You wouldn't." Violet gasped in horror. Confused, I looked between the two.

"What? You don't understand?" Juliette taunted me in a whiny voice. "You see this little map holds the key to my wealth. Once Peter digs it up and hands me the diamond, he will accidentally, of course, fall into the active volcano, along with you two." She waved the knife between us. "And the little map. Then I go back to living my life without the burden of a man that really never loved me or his homeless, parentless brother, who by the way was supposed to burn up along with his parents."

"You killed them?" Violet shook. "You are the one who blew up their house?"

"How else was I going to shut Patrick's father up from telling him who I really was?" She waved her finger across her neck. "First I slit their throats. Then I took the map before I turned on the gas stove. I set the perfect backdraft so when Patrick and I came home that night and opened the door, the house would explode."

The thoughts of what happened entered my mind so quickly, it was hard to put them together. But the one thing I knew, I was wrong. Violet hadn't killed Patrick, Juliette had, over some sort of diamond.

"It was all planned out. I had the map that Patrick thought his brother had drawn, but I knew better. I'd heard of the myth of the diamond at Tulip Island and I did a little research. You really shouldn't put photos and names of your tourists on your site because I knew I could get my claws into Patrick. I moved across the states and made sure I was everything he wanted in a woman. Caring toward his brother and all too happy to take guardianship of Peter. Now that Patrick is dead, Peter will be sent off to an institute where he will rot forever. Or. . ." she glanced back. "Like I said, dig for the treasure only to slip and fall after the diamond is safely in my hands."

"Why did you kill his parents?" Violet wanted all the answers while I just wanted to get out of there.

"Peter! Come on! It's time to get the treasure." Her voice echoed loud and clear as the rain stopped.

Off in the distance, the lightning and storm seemed to have blown off.

"It was really the father I wanted. I want the P&P stores and all the jewels. I want wealth. The money. But when he rejected my womanly offerings, he told me that he was going to tell Patrick about me trying to seduce him and that I only wanted Patrick for the money." A smile curled on her lips. "He was a fool. He told me that I had twenty-four hours to break it off with Patrick and go away quietly or he was going to tell Patrick. Plus, it didn't help that it was on camera where I'd been snooping around for the map." She drew her hands in the air, the knife dangling. "The rest is history."

Peter shuffled up past me.

"Don't do this, Peter." I glanced down at my cat in hopes he'd stop Peter somehow.

Peter stopped for a brief second.

"Come Peter." Juliette encouraged him. "You can help me find the treasure."

Peter nodded. The wet hoodie clung to his head. I could feel the panic rising from my gut to my throat. I rubbed my finger and my thumb together, trying to get my thoughts in order so I could cast the right spell from my finger.

Before I could even put a thought together, Peter was next to her. He grabbed her by the wrists and tried to bring her to the ground. She flailed. The knife went flying. Her nails ripped at Peter's eyes, ripping the hoodie off of his head.

"Oscar!" I screamed and scurried over to the edge of the volcano. The lava shot into the air like a cannon, exploding into the sky. "Oscar!"

It was apparent that Oscar had seen Peter and switched clothes, but how was I going to save him. I couldn't string two words together, much less a thought spell.

I shot a look back at Mr. Prince Charming; he was doing figure eights around Violet's ankles. She lifted her arms in the air. A swirl of neon orange lifted out of the volcano. In the bottom of the swirl was the diamond. The treasure. Violet brought her hands together, a thunderous clap echoed, shattering the diamond into tiny specks of dust.

Juliette had let go of Oscar. He crawled to safety as she tried to grab the diamond dust out of the air.

"No!" she screamed out and leaned a little too far over the edge. The swirl circled her and she disappeared into the depths of the volcano.

Chapter Seventeen

"I hope you have enjoyed your stay on Tulip Island." Mr. Victor stayed his pleasant self even after Juliette had killed Patrick and fallen to her death in the active volcano.

The sea was once again calm. The full moon was out and the stars once again dotted the amazing tropical sky. The tiki torches were lit and the food smelled divine.

"The past couple of days have been really nice." Oscar was such a gentleman after nearly losing his life.

After we'd all come back down from the volcano, everything had made sense. Mr. Victor was like Darla. He'd met Violet's mother who was a Fairiwick like Eloise. They'd lived in a village and Violet's mother died during childbirth with Violet. She wasn't built to have mortal children and her body gave out on her. Like me and Darla, the council from his village allowed him to move Violet out of the village as long as they kept an eye on him.

That was when he'd decided to live alone on Tulip Island. That was how the Elders knew to send me and Oscar there on our honeymoon, only they didn't factor in that crime happens everywhere.

Mr. Victor had tried his best to shield Violet from the world, but a young Patrick had stolen her heart and given her a child. Only at an early age, Mr. Victor could tell that Gene was not mortal. He too had gotten his mother's spiritual gift and was a wizard like Oscar.

Violet was unable to keep it a secret when she saw Patrick that they had a son. Patrick told her that he wasn't going to marry Juliette and he and Peter were going to stay on the island with her, Gene, and Mr. Victor. Patrick told Juliette that he wasn't going to marry her when he'd returned from the night snorkeling excursion. After he told her, he grabbed his scuba equipment to do a quick dive on the coral reef right beyond the shoreline. Juliette snorkeled her way over and cut the scuba tube, drowning Patrick.

But not before she'd stolen my brush from the beach and took out Violet's red hair strands and planted them on Patrick. She had the perfect plan and thought she was going to get away with it.

The local police had recovered Juliette's charred body from the erupted volcano and had taken Oscar's statement about her killing Patrick to gain his fortune. The case was solved and closed.

Mr. Victor and the Order of Elders were nice enough to give Oscar and I a few days alone on the island while Violet and Peter recuperated. Constance and Patience, along with Mr. Prince Charming, were sent back to Whispering Falls. Tonight was finally our tiki dinner.

"We have very much enjoyed the last couple of days." I reached over the table and placed my hand on top of Oscar's. "You've made us feel very welcome."

"I guess we are all sort of family." Mr. Victor nodded, leaving Oscar and I to enjoy what little time we had left on the island.

Which wasn't a long time. Our bags were packed and we were taking the red-eye straight back to Whispering Falls. It was by choice because I didn't want Oscar to look out of the plane's window and down into the ocean. And I couldn't help but put a little Mr. Sandman Sprinkles in his dinner cocktail.

It might've been illegal to do in Whispering Falls, but not on Tulip Island and it was for the sake of our marriage.

"Are you ready?" Gene walked up to us. He held our bags in each of his hands. "The plane has landed on the beach and everyone is waiting to see you off."

Oscar stood up and helped me out of my chair. He stood behind me with his arms around my waist and we looked out at the ocean. He rested his chin on top of my head. I could feel his heart beating on my back.

"Even though we had a little snafu, I still enjoyed our time." He gave me a squeeze.

"Thank you for taking me to see the ocean and letting me put my toes in the sand." I wiggled my bare feet underneath me, feeling the grain.

Hand-in-hand, Oscar and I followed Gene to the propeller plane where we'd make our connection to the red-eye once we got on the mainland.

Just like he said, Mr. Victor, Violet, and Peter were standing on the shore waiting for us.

"So all that potion and stuff was because you are a real witch?" Violet asked.

"It is. Just like you." I ran my hand down her arm. "It's an exciting time for you, now that Mr. Victor is no longer taking mortal tourists, you can use your spiritual gift."

I didn't know what her gift was and I wasn't quite sure she knew. The one thing I did know was that Mr. Victor had promised her that he'd tell her all about her mom and make sure it wasn't too late for Gene to learn about his true spiritual calling.

Peter was going to stay on the island with Mr. Victor who would adopt him like Madame Torres had predicted, only I was so caught up in finding something bad about Mr. Victor, I failed at using my intuitional gift of seeking out the good. I made a promise to myself that I was going to get better at that.

I buried my toes one last time in the sand before I stepped on the plane and put on my shoes. I had a sneaky suspicion that I wasn't going to be coming back to the beach for a long time.

Chapter Eighteen

The faint ring of the chains brought me out of my sleep. Oscar was happily snoring away in our bed and it felt so good to wake up and be home. The Karima sisters had picked us up at the airport in the middle of the night and they were still fussing about nothing important.

After they dropped us off at our cottage, I loved on Mr. Prince Charming and decided to leave the unpacking for the morning. Only I didn't want to unpack. I wanted to run down the hill and watch Eloise bless the town that I loved and missed so much.

I quickly put on a pair of capri jeans, a white tee-shirt, and slipped on some flats. I couldn't wait to tell Eloise about our trip. I loved this time of the morning when the burnt orange sun was peeking over the mountains, the sunlight putting its first touch on Whispering Falls and when Eloise blessed each and every shop.

The sound of the chains connected to her incense burner echoed down Main Street and up the hill with each swing. The smell of lavender and sage filled the air. A cleansing smell. It was an elegant exciting smell that told me I was home and safe.

Mr. Prince Charming darted around the buildings before I even reached the back of A Charming Cure. I ran my hand along the side of my shop and felt the sheer energy go into my fingertips. My honeymoon might've started out a little stressful, but I was energized and ready to get back to work.

When I turned the corner between my shop and Magical Moments, there was a crowd gathered down near Bella's Baubles. I made my way to the front and found Izzy, Gerald, Petunia, and Chandra standing behind Eloise. Baby Orin cooed from the pouch hooked on Gerald's back. I patted his hiney.

Eloise wore a long green cloak that was pulled over her head. She swung the incense side-to-side in a fluid motion. Smoke barreled out on the downswing sending the smoke up into what looked to be a new business coming to town.

"Fortune, health, and wealth," she chanted in a monotone voice. "Fortune, health, and wealth."

It was pretty much the same cleansing ceremony she did every morning, but this morning she was focusing on the new shop.

I turned around when I felt a hand on my back. Petunia nodded for me to follow her along with the rest.

"How was the end of your trip?" Petunia asked. She tilted her head to the side and an empty bird's nest fell out. Everyone looked down at the ground. "They left the nest this morning."

"My trip was wonderful." I wanted to keep some things to myself. "And you wouldn't believe that Tulip Island is run by a mortal man who has a Fairiwick for a daughter."

"Oh yes we would." Petunia took a step forward and the crowd parted.

The newest shop in Whispering Falls was complete. Instead of a sidewalk walking up to the shop and entering through the ornamental gate, there was a wooden swinging bridge that led you through the ornamental gate and up to the red cottage shop. The red and purple awning flapped in the morning wind. Hidden Treasures was written in yellow and in the front display window was a shelf full of what-knots, candles, and frames along with a dress form. There was a dress on display that I'd seen before but couldn't place.

The front door of the shop was in the shape of a sewing needle and instead of the oval shape where thread would feed through, it was in the shape of the sun.

Everyone stood silent as the door opened and a young boy popped out alongside the cutest red-headed, freckled-faced woman.

"Welcome to Whispering Falls, we are a charming community." Petunia took her job as Village President very seriously. She pulled a copy of the by-laws out of her cloak as she walked across the bridge and handed the manual over. "On behalf of the village council, we'd like to invite you to your first smudging ceremony tonight at dusk at The Gathering Rock."

The sunshine broke over Gene's face and he stared at me, a big smile on his face.

"Hi, June!" he called and waved. I smiled and waved back.

Mr. Prince Charming darted across the bridge and did figure eights around Gene's ankles.

Everyone clapped to welcome our newest resident—as everyone knows that Mr. Prince Charming was the real welcoming committee.

About the Author

For years, *USA Today* bestselling author Tonya Kappes has been self-publishing her numerous mystery and romance titles with unprecedented success. She is famous not only for her hilarious plotlines and quirky characters, but her tremendous marketing efforts that have earned her thousands of followers and a devoted street team of fans. Be sure to check out Tonya's website for upcoming events and news and to sign up for her newsletter! Tonyakappes.com

Also by Tonya Kappes

Olivia Davis Paranormal Mystery Series
SPLITSVILLE.COM
COLOR ME LOVE (novella)
COLOR ME A CRIME

Magical Cures Mystery Series
A CHARMING CRIME
A CHARMING CURE
A CHARMING POTION (novella)
A CHARMING WISH
A CHARMING SPELL
A CHARMING MAGIC
A CHARMING SECRET
A CHARMING CHRISTMAS (novella)
A CHARMING FATALITY
A CHARMING GHOST
A CHARMING HEX
A CHARMING VOODOO (Fall 2016)

Grandberry Falls Series
THE LADYBUG JINX
HAPPY NEW LIFE
A SUPERSTITIOUS CHRISTMAS (novella)
NEVER TELL YOUR DREAMS

A Laurel London Mystery Series
CHECKERED CRIME
CHECKERED PAST
CHECKERED THIEF

A Divorced Diva Beading Mystery Series
A BREAD OF DOUBT SHORT STORY
STRUNG OUT TO DIE
CRIMPED TO DEATH

Bluegrass Romance Series
GROOMING MR. RIGHT
TAMING MR. RIGHT

Women's Fiction
CARPE BREAD 'EM

Young Adult
TAG YOU'RE IT

A Ghostly Southern Mystery Series
A GHOSTLY UNDERTAKING
A GHOSTLY GRAVE
A GHOSTLY DEMISE
A GHOSTLY MURDER
A GHOSTLY REUNION (available for presale)
A GHOSTLY MORTALITY (available for presale)

Copyright

54203425R00086

Made in the USA
Middletown, DE
02 December 2017